THE RAVEN HAIRED ROGUE

THE RAVEN HAIRED ROGUE

A NOVELLA

John M. Zakour

ISBN: 0692444378
ISBN 13: 9780692444375
Library of Congress Control Number: 2015907359
Serealities Press, Birmingham, AL

My name is Zachary Nixon Johnson. My beat is New Frisco. It's the year 2057, and I'm the last freelance private investigator on Earth. Yeah, I know that might sound a little ominous to some and kind of cool to others, but truthfully it's not ominous at all. No catastrophe killed off the other freelance PIs. It's just that these days, everything is wired to everything else. Information is readily available for just the cost of a few seconds of time on a search engine and a surcharge of a few credits. Your average first grader can dig up more information in a nanosecond than the best-connected PI could have done just a few decades ago.

That doesn't mean people still don't need PIs. After all, some information can be especially tricky to obtain. You know, the type of information that needs a special kind of extra poking and prodding around. The type of prodding that requires a personal touch and what I like to call extra sensitive persuasiveness. I call it that because it often requires finding a person's sensitive spot and jarring it. So yep, even in this modern mega tech world there is still a demand for our services. In fact, being a PI can be quite profitable at times.

That's the other catch to being a freelance PI. If there's a nice profit to be made, you can bet big business will find a way to siphon off as much of those credits as possible. Today, there are two big private investigation companies. There's DickCo., which is run by entertainment ultra mega corporation Entercorp. And there's EyesRUs, owned by technology giant HTech. A PI's life can be filled with violence and danger, making it a natural fit for the entertainment industry and reality HV. HTech jumped in the game after it figured out that technology goes out of date, but lust and greed never do. Both of these big PI companies have the same MO. Potential clients contact them via their net sites. Then, if the company finds the client's plight interesting (i.e., marketable) enough, it will send out a team—all of which is broadcast live over one of the reality HV channels. Certainly takes the *private* out of *private investigator*, but some folks eat it up. Lucky for me, some clients still like to keep things more tight-lipped—which means I do get work. And when work arrives, it's usually quite interesting.

Today is a slow day. I'm sitting back in my real-leather chair in my office by the bay. I'm recounting the tale of one of my early PI adventures to my holographic assistant, HARV, and my flesh-and-blood assistant, Carol.

"There I was in the crowded theater looking for the e-blackmailer, and a mime and an android dressed as a mime were heading toward the crowd. I knew the mime was harmless, but the android had a bomb. I only had seconds to decide which one to take out..."

"So what did you do, tió?" Carol asks. I should note that Carol is the niece of my fiancée, Dr. Electra Gevada. Carol has the same beauty, charm, and temper as her aunt.

"I shot 'em both with a heavy electric stun charge," I tell her. "Turns out I got more praise for stopping the actual mime than I did the android."

HARV looks at me and yawns. "You don't have to be me, the most sophisticated cognitive processor on Earth, to know that mimes are truly annoying."

HARV may have a bit of an ego, but he was most likely correct on both accounts. Mimes can be quite annoying, and HARV was probably the most sophisticated computer around. Yeah sure, these days pretty much everybody over the age of three wears a Portable Interactive Holographic Interface Personally Optimized Device, or a P-Pod for short. And yep, these devices do allow easy access to a constant wealth of information. Sure, they even all have their own rudimentary personalities, such as the Bob, Betty, Bunny, and Bubba models.

Thing is, none of these canned artificial personalities are a changing, constantly evolving intelligence like HARV is. Turns out most people are very uneasy about having a computer interface that has more personality than they do. Of course, it doesn't help that HARV can be a bit sarcastic at times. Plus the fact that he loves to appear as a snobbish, balding British butler doesn't exactly endear HARV to the average Joe or Jane Doe.

Oh, I should mention that HARV is physically connected to my brain. Having an ultra mega supercomputer wired to my cerebral cortex lets me have constant access to pretty much all the information in the known worlds. It allows HARV to tap into my body and the underarmor I wear to let me move faster, take more damage, and punch harder than other humans. I can project holograms from my left-eye lens, which is pretty subzero. On the downside, I have a nosy supercomputer constantly critiquing my every move.

Carol's bright-green eyes pop open. She puts her fingers to her forehead and leans forward, her long, golden-brown hair dropping down her shoulders. I swear she starts to glow with energy. I should note that Carol is a class I level VII psi, which means she can do things with her mind that most people only dream of.

"Zach, I'm picking up a vibe. You are about to get a call from the Kardasian Towers hotel. The vibe's message isn't totally clear. But I do know he, she, or it wants you to find a dog from Mars."

"I don't usually find dogs, even ones from Mars," I note.

"From what I understand, the client wants to pay a million credits," Carol tells me.

"Of course, there is a first for everything," I say.

"Zach, you have a call coming in from Merinda-1616," HARV tells me. "Do you wish to accept it as a hologram or on the wall screen?"

This is obviously the vibe Carol had.

I take my feet off my real-oak desk. I sit up and straighten my jacket. Even though my office is meant to look much like the typical gumshoe's office from a hundred years ago, looks can be deceiving. I have all the modern necessities: wall screens equipped with full-room holographic projectors and a laser defense system. (Believe me, when you're me, a laser defense system is a necessity.) I point to my left wall. "Left wall screen, please."

The image of a regal-looking woman with long black hair fills my left wall. Her dark hair is made more striking by her creamy-white skin. She holds her head high, and her piercing green eyes are locked on the screen, unwavering. She is probably a little older than I am, but not much.

"Mr. Johnson, thank you for taking my call. I am Merinda-1616. I am part of the High Council of Mars."

A message from HARV rolls across my eyes. "Remember Zach, people from Mars, well Martians, all use numbers for last names. They believe it gives them solidarity."

"The pleasure is mine, Merinda. What brings you to Earth?"

"I am here trying to negotiate a trade deal between Earth and the Mars colony. As I am sure you are aware, we on Mars make the finest handcrafted goods in the known worlds," she tells me without batting an eyelash.

"Yes," I say with a nod. I point to Carol. "My assistant, Carol, has one of your scarves that she raves about." I lean toward the screen and ask, "So to what do I owe the pleasure of your call?"

"I want to hire you to find my dog and dearest companion, Saturn," she tells me. "He's a special creature."

I sit back in my chair and prop my hands behind my head. "Oh?"

Merinda nods. "Yes, very special. His IQ is well over two hundred, and he can communicate telepathically."

"Now, that is special," I say. "When did he go missing?"

"A couple of hours ago. He said this hotel was too stuffy and that he needed some fresh air. He left, and that's the last I heard from him." She shivers a little. "I wanted to send a security person with him, but he insisted that he's a big boy." Her eyes plead to the screen. "Please, Zach, you have to find him. I'll pay a hundred thousand credits in advance and another hundred thousand credits when you find him."

OK, not exactly the million credits Carol thought it would be, but even the best psis aren't perfect. Besides, two hundred thousand credits to track down a dog isn't a bad payday.

"Sure, I'll do it," I tell her.

Her eyes pop open, and her lips curl into a smile. "I'm staying on the thirteenth floor of the Kardasian Towers. Come here, and I will give you all of Saturn's pertinent information."

"Sounds like a plan," I say. "When tracking down a subject, it's always helpful to see his or her last-known surroundings. I may get a clue." I stand up from my desk. "I should be there in twenty minutes."

"I look forward to meeting you," Merinda says. She nods, and my wall screen goes blank.

I turn to Carol. "Ready for a little road trip?"

"Sorry, I was wrong about the amount," she says.

I shrug. "Nobody is perfect. Not even you."

I walk over to my actual-wood coatrack and take my fedora off the top.

"Why must you insist on always wearing that hat when you start a case?" HARV asks.

"It helps set the proper tone," I insist, walking out the door. "Being a PI is as much about attitude as anything else."

It's a nice sunny day on the New Frisco pier. A few tourists dot the street, taking 3-D photos of themselves standing by the water, like that's some great accomplishment. Three other tourists—a man, a woman, and a kid—are ogling my 1973 cherry-red Mustang. Now, these are people with taste.

"Is this really your vehicle, sir?" the kid asks. He's a small kid with red hair and freckles.

"It is," I say with a grin.

"And you actually have to drive it yourself?" the mom asks, her hair done up in a near-perfect bun.

"I do," I say.

"How quaint and archaic," the dad says. I notice he has an old pipe in his front pocket, which is weird. Hardly anybody smokes these days, especially not from a 1950s-style pipe.

"HARV, scan these folks," I think. "They look too much like a 1950s sitcom family to be real."

HARV appears, projecting himself from my wrist communicator. "First off, the car has been modified so I can drive it if needed. Second, Zach, these people are all wearing holographic disguises."

The kid looks at HARV and smiles. "Wow, you really are as good as people say."

The three family members each touch a button on his or her respective belt. The holographic covers blur away. I am now standing face-to-face—well, face-to-chest—with three big apes in really expensive suits.

Oh, I'm not talking dramatically here. These are three actual apes. These days if some companies have messages they want to deliver in a hard-to-ignore package, they use actual apes. Apes are big and intimidating, and they haven't unionized like human and mutant muscle. Plus, they are easier to maintain than android muscle. And when push comes to shove, apes are scarier than androids. Still, I'm not one to scare easily.

I lock eyes with the biggest ape, figuring he or she is the leader—my thought process being that I could stare him or her down.

"Dude," the ape I'm locking eyes with says. "We each outweigh you by a good one hundred kilos, and we're freaking apes carrying heat."

The other two apes open their jackets to reveal very big sidearms.

"Your point being?" I snarl.

The lead ape points to his ear. "Plus, we're each wearing really expensive psi blockers, so Carol can't warp us with her mind."

"Your point being?" I repeat.

The lead ape opens up his arms and lifts his hands. It's meant to be a friendly gesture. "We just want to talk…"

"Zach, I've tapped into the apes' communication devices," HARV tells me in my mind. "They seem to be in the employment of a new reality HV network called Actual, Real Reality HV Net."

Now would be a good time to mention that the reality networks all want to sign me. They figure the network that reels in the last freelance PI will get a major ratings boost. In a way, it's a bit flattering, but in practice, it's far more annoying. I want these apes to back down. They say they just want to talk, but the thing is they are apes, and apes respect a show of power. I do wear reinforced, HARV-enhanced underarmor and keep a nifty Colt-4500 up my sleeve. I am more than capable of holding my own in a brawl, even if it's against three apes. Still, years in the business have taught me there are times when you get more out of making the right gesture than throwing a right cross.

I hold up my palms to the apes. It's a friendly gesture meant to show them I mean no harm.

"Listen, guys, I'm flattered," I tell them. "But like I told all your competition, I am not doing reality HV."

The three apes look at one another and then burst out laughing. The two apes in back are actually hitting their thighs—they're laughing so hard.

"Ah, what's so funny?" I ask.

The lead ape straightens up, composing himself just a little. He adjusts his pink tie as he tells me, "Dude, we don't want you. We're not just the muscle here. We're also the brains of this new HV network. We see things differently than humans. You're old news and, well, old. What are you, forty now? We are targeting a young subzero demographic." He points to Carol and HARV. "We want them. The girl is beautiful, so guys will dig her; yet she is powerful, so women will get behind her. Plus, she has that IT factor. The hologram—well, he's the perfect snooty sidekick. People will love to hate him."

"He's far from perfect," I note.

"I am not snooty. I am confident in my knowledge," HARV remarks, head tossed back. "I am also definitely *not* a sidekick."

"I like to keep my life as private as possible," Carol says.

The ape nods his head. "I get it. I understand not wanting to stand out."

"This coming from a big ape in a pink suit," I note.

The ape looks me in the eyes. "Our suits and ties have interactive nano-colors that we can adjust for the circumstance. We thought the pink would be friendlier." He shakes his head. "But that's neither here nor there. My point is that our terms are very reasonable and generous." He touches the P-Pod on his ear, and a holographic contract appears. "All you have to do is live your lives and let us record it."

HARV crosses his arms. "I've scanned the terms. They are reasonable, but Carol and I are not a sideshow. When you do what we do, it's best to stay private. That's why they call us *private* eyes…"

The ape points to me. "Technically and legally, he's the only PI. We would call the show the *Last Girl Friday*."

"Catchy title," I admit.

"Sorry, guys, no deal," Carol says.

The lead ape nods. "I understand. If you change your mind, you have our contact info."

The apes turn and walk away.

"Smart choice," I tell Carol and HARV.

"Please, it's a start-up company run by apes," HARV says. "Carol and I would be better off self-recording and broadcasting our adventures over the net."

I look at him.

"Not that we would do that," HARV adds.

"Between this and my other side job, I really cherish my privacy," Carol says.

I should note that much to my chagrin, Carol also works as sort of an unofficial Earth spokesperson/representative to the Gladians. They are a race of aliens that made contact with Earth way back in 2022. They shared with us all sorts of their technology, and all they've asked from us so far is for our dirt and our chocolate chip cookies. They mostly leave us alone. In fact, today very few average Jane and John Does have even seen a Gladian. .

I get into my car and head toward the Kardasian Towers, or the KT as people like to be called.

2

The KT is not all that much to look at, just two bland, side-by-side towers stretching up fifty or so stories. The only truly distinguishing features they have are the domes that dot the top of each tower. These domes give the onlooker (well, at least me) the impression that the towers have a giant butt on top of them—which is kind of fitting, since the KT is an ultra mega high-priced hotel set in what passes for the butt end of Frisco. Its motto is, "For special folks who want to mingle with the little people." Yeah, it's not very catchy. It's meant to be a semi-ironic hotel—a place where people with too many credits can overspend these credits and not really get anything much back in return. To me, the most ironic thing, is with Frisco being the crown city of Earth, even the butt end is pretty shiny and fairly safe.

Entering the KT's main lobby, the walls and ceiling are bright white and covered with glitter. The lobby itself, though, is perfectly barren—no front desk, no bellhops, no anything.

"The KT is an upscale, no-frills hotel," HARV tells me. "Its clientele like to rough it…"

"So for five thousand credits a night, they get no services?" I say.

"Yep, part of the appeal," HARV tells me. He points to the left. "The elevator is this way. Of course their brouchre says the elevator is only for old farts who won't take the stairs…"

We come to a long white hallway that has to stretch one hundred meters.

"The elevator is at the end." HARV says, stretching his arm down the hall.

We start walking down the hallway. "Why did they have to put the elevator so far away?"

"They do it so the guests don't feel pampered," HARV says. "It's all part of the appeal."

We start walking down the long hallway. I hear a buzz behind me. Looking over my shoulder, I see a little, round cleaning robot has come out of its station in the wall. It is trailing us.

"Apparently, the little cleaning bot thinks we're going to make a mess," I joke.

"I am a hologram. I can't make a mess," HARV says. "Carol is quite neat, but you, Zach, can be a bit of a slob. I am guessing the cleaning bots at your office and home have relayed this information to all the cleaning bots in the area."

I shrug and keep walking. I can't help but notice the buzzing sound growing louder. Looking over my shoulder again, I now see there are two more cleaning bots behind the first one. All three bots are following us.

"I'm not that bad!" I insist as we keep walking.

"Tió, you can cause a lot of damage," Carol tells me. "The bots just probably want to be prepared."

I see three more bots come out of their stations on the floor. These three bots take position behind the others. The buzzing sound increases.

"OK, this is getting ridiculous!" I say.

"Zach, the last time you were in an upscale hotel, you got into a gunfight with assassins and a couple of superwomen causing extensive damage. You cannot blame these bots for being overly cautious," HARV says.

Calling over my shoulder, I tell the bots, "I'm just here to talk to a client."

I can't help but notice there are now ten cleaning bots in bowling-pin formation trailing us.

"I gotta admit this is weird even for us," Carol says, glancing over her shoulder.

"Please, you humans are just overreacting," HARV insists.

Then as if on cue, the ten cleaning bots murmur, "Kill, crush, clean!"

"OK, maybe not such an overreaction," HARV admits.

I stop walking and turn and face the round little bots. "OK, this is ridiculous. What are you planning to do? Suck me to death?"

"Actually, Zach, these bots are equipped with laser-clean technology, to burn off the really tough spots. I calculate with a slight adjustment they could cause harm," HARV says.

The lead bot hovers up off the ground, exposing its underbelly to me. A laser beam from the middle of the bot hits me in the shoulder. My underarmor prevents the blast from reaching my skin, but it still burns through my suit.

"See!" HARV tells me. "It is good to be right."

I don't mind being attacked now and then. It comes with the job. But I take offense when a person, mutant, animal, or bot rips my suit. That's just so uncool.

I now notice that the other nine bots are also hovering in the air, positioning themselves to fire on me.

"Do you want me to help, tió?" Carol asks. "Or do you want to handle these bots yourself…"

I look at the little cleaning bots, the ten of them hovering up in the hotel hallway. They certainly don't look all that menacing. But as the hole in my suit proves, these days you don't have to look dangerous to be dangerous.

"Listen bots, I don't want trouble," I say. "Stand down now!"

"They are cleaning bots. They won't pay any attention to you. They have something they need to clean up, and they will not stop until that job is done. I am actually trying to override their programming," HARV tells me. "It's not easy because they are such simple machines. They are simply programmed to see a spot and remove that spot."

"So they think of me as a dirt spot?" I ask.

"Apparently so," HARV says. "I've been able to confound them so far, which has prevented them from shooting at you again, but I calculate I can't hold them much longer. It's like trying to deal with a bunch of dimwits. You can distract them for a moment with a bright, shiny object, but sooner rather than later, they will get bored with it and move on."

I move my left wrist in just the right way that makes my trusty Colt-4500 pop into my hand. I wave my gun at the bots.

"Now back off, bots!" I order.

HARV puts his hands on his hips and sighs. "Zach, these bots will not listen to you. They are very single-minded. I also should note that there are no security cameras in this hotel. Apparently, the patrons value their privacy more than security."

"Probably because they travel with their own security," I suggest.

"Noted. The point being, if you fire your gun because you claim you are being attacked by harmless cleaning bots, there will be some doubts," HARV tells me.

I think about the situation. Firing my gun in public is never a good thing. Sure, the hotel isn't that crowded, but with my luck, some overly pampered customer would show up the minute I pulled the trigger. Plus, the authorities are never fans of me shooting up a place for no apparent reason. Sure, in this case I had a reason, but I'm not sure they'd believe that the cleaning bots were attacking me.

"Kill, crush, clean!" the ten bots echo as one.

"Carol, take them out," I say.

"With pleasure," Carol says with a smile.

Carol points at the bots and then gestures to the left. The ten bots go crashing into the left hall wall. Carol swipes her arm to the right. The bots fly from the left wall and slam into the right wall. The bots shatter into hundreds of little bot pieces. The pieces sprinkle harmlessly to the ground.

"I wonder who will clean up this mess," Carol says.

"Not our problem," I tell her.

We head to the elevator and up to Merinda's floor.

3

My experience has taught me that dignitaries like to have lots of aides and servants around. It gives them an air of importance. Therefore, I'm surprised when Merinda greets us at her hotel room door.

"Zach, I'm so glad you came," Merinda says as she opens the door. "Please come in so I can update you on my situation."

Carol, HARV, and I walk into the room. It's a big area. The walls are painted a bright, shiny, almost-glowing yellow. But outside of that, not much else separates it from your standard hotel room. I am surprised to see the only person in the room with Merinda is a small lady with gray hair and big eyes.

Merinda motions to the small lady. "This is my aide, Alicia. She is constantly by my side."

"I assume you travel with more than just one aide and a dog," I coax.

Merinda nods, lowering her eyes ever so slightly. "Yes, the rest of my staff is out looking for Saturn. But Alicia will not leave me alone."

This is the second time in less than a minute that Merinda has noted how her aide is sticking by her. I get the feeling from Merinda's words and actions that she wants some alone time with me. She just can't say it out loud. I need to put Alicia on ice, at least for a few moments, so Merinda can speak freely.

"Carol, can you stun Alicia for a second?" I think to Carol.

Carol focuses on Alicia and squints her eyes. Alicia stands there nervously looking at us.

"I can't get a lock on her brain," Carol thinks back to me. "It's weird. It's like she's immune to my powers…"

OK, so it looks like we will have to deal with Merinda under Alicia's watchful eyes, at least for now.

"So when was the last time you saw your dog?" I ask Merinda, getting right to the business at hand.

"Zach, he's an intelligent creature. He is my friend and companion, but not mine to own."

I clear my throat. "When was the last time you saw Saturn, *the* dog?"

Alicia steps forward. "We saw him exactly two hours and forty-two minutes ago."

Merinda shakes her head a bit nervously. I can tell she is clearly worried about something. I'm just not totally positive it's her dog. "The very worrisome thing is I haven't heard anything from him, either."

"Does he have some sort of communication device?" I ask.

Merinda shakes her head. "No, we have a mental bond," she tells me. "He can broadcast his thoughts to me…"

"Of course he can," I say. This wouldn't be a job for me, if this were just a normal superintelligent dog.

"Is there a range limit on your mental link?" Carol asks.

"Why doesn't Saturn wear a GPS locator?" HARV asks and scolds at the same time.

Merinda looks at Carol and smiles. "Saturn and I have never been more than a few kilometers apart, and we've always been able to maintain our link." She looks at HARV and frowns. "He does not wear a locator because he is an intelligent being who does not wish to wear a locator."

Her annoyance at HARV makes me smile just a little. "Take me to Saturn's room or pillow or whatever…" I say. "I'll also need an image of him."

Merinda points to a door at the far end of the room. "He sleeps on a cushion on the floor of my room. Plus, I have a photo of the two of us together there."

"Let's see them," I say, walking toward the door. "Has he acted unusual the last few days?"

Merinda follows me toward the room, with Alicia on her tail like a persistant shadow. "Not really. He was looking forward to coming to Earth. He's never been here. He said he was excited to breathe in a real atmosphere—not a man-made one, like on Mars."

"Can't blame him," I say.

"Oh, please," HARV says. "The terraformed Mars atmosphere isn't all that different from Earth's. It's actually one of the greatest achievements of humankind."

"Thanks to the Gladians," Alicia adds.

"Of course," HARV agrees. "Pretty much all of Earth's mega leap in technology is due to the Gladians."

"Didn't the Gladians actually terraform a part of Mars before they made contact with us?" I say.

HARV looks at me with wide-open eyes. "Yes, that is correct."

"I know stuff," I say.

"The Gladians were always interested in human DNA," Alicia says. "They did establish a small base on Mars before they made contact with most of Earth, just in case. They wanted to make sure the human race survived." She pauses. "But the complete terraforming of Mars was a combined effort."

"Alicia is quite the historian," Merinda notes.

Interesting how the Gladians have always had such an interest in human DNA. Of course, that is something to ponder at a later date. Now that we are in the bedroom, it's time to focus on matters at hand.

Saturn's dog cushion is a big, light-brown, fluffy pillow. It does look comfy, even to my human eyes. On top of the pillow is an old, bright-red ball. I bend down and pick up the ball. It is soft and makes a squeaking sound when squeezed. I guess a really intelligent dog is still a dog. Right next to the pillow are two old paper magazines, a *Field and Stream* and a *Popular Electronics*.

"So he likes to read old-fashioned paper," I note out loud.

Merinda nods. "Yes, it's expensive as anything, but Saturn asks for so little and gives so much. He says holographic and electronic displays give him a headache if he looks at them too long."

"I can identify with that," I say.

Merinda grabs a photo off of her nightstand and shows it to me. It's a shot of her holding a medium-size, golden-brown, perfectly groomed collie. She points to the collie. "This is Saturn," she says.

"Yeah, I kind of figured that out." Pointing at the picture, I say, "You're also quite strong to be carrying around a thirty-plus–kilo dog."

"I work out," Merinda tells me with a smile.

"Zach, I have been scanning all security camera data in the area. I have no sign of Saturn…" HARV tells me.

"Not surprising. He's too low to the ground for most cameras to pick up."

This is going to take some old-fashioned legwork. I figure I have two places to start. He is a dog, and I get the feeling he longs for open space and green grass, so a nearby park is certainly a possibility. But he is also quite intelligent, so I can't rule out the possibility he would go to a museum. Of course, a dog would certainly stand out more in a museum than in a park. And of course, this isn't your average dog. Nevertheless, as the ball proved, you can add intelligence to the dog, but it is still a dog.

ooking at Saturn's little dog area, I decide that the dog part of him must overwhelm his non-dog side.

"HARV, where's the nearest park?" I ask.

"HTech's new and improved Golden Gate Park," HARV says, pointing out the window. "It's only a few blocks away. It is a very fine park. It even has a museum and an aquarium." HARV morphs into the animated image of a green park. There are people walking to and fro. "This is a live image of the park now from satellite data. No sign of Saturn. Of course, it might be hard to identify a specific dog from this height. There are no security cameras or drones, since the park is designated a low technology zone. Even P-Pods and communicators must be put on mute." HARV shivers a little. He shakes his head. "I still don't quite comprehend the need for such places…"

"Sometimes we humans want breaks to collect our thoughts and commune with nature. It makes us closer to our ancestors," I say. "We need to tune out the electronic noise."

I look at Merinda. "We're going to check out Golden Gate Park. I'll let you know if we find him. I assume you will contact us if he returns here."

Merinda nods. "Of course." She leans forward and hugs me. I gotta admit—I like it. "Zach, I really appreciate this."

I pull back and look her in those eyes. "I just hope you feel the same way when you get my bill."

Merinda smiles.

Carol, HARV, and I head out of the room.

We arrive at the north entrance of Golden Gate Park. It's a wide-open green space, dotted with a few park benches. Redbrick walking paths neatly dissect all the green spots. Assorted people are sitting, standing, and pretty much just hanging out. A couple of kids are flying kites. A bunch of teens are kicking a soccer ball back and forth. A young father is hitting a baseball to his kids. A few couples are sitting, having a picnic lunch. A kid floats by on a hover board.

"There is a nice pond about eight hundred twenty-one meters to the south," HARV says as we stroll through the park. "That is a very popular hangout spot."

As we walk, I scan the area for dogs. There are a lot of them. I guess when you have a city where green space is sparse, it's only natural for owners to want to bring their pets to the most natural place possible.

"There are a lot of dogs here," I say.

HARV looks at me. "Zach, I've counted thirty-three dogs within a one-hundred-meter radius. None of them match Saturn's description. This park covers two thousand seventeen acres. Searching it manually for a small moving dog is going to prove most difficult. Not as difficult as, say, finding a needle in a haystack." HARV rubs his chin. "I would more equate the difficulty level to finding a baseball bat in a haystack that is moving." HARV shakes his head. "What I am trying to say is currently our finding him would be more of a matter of luck than of skill."

Yeah, I'm not one to rely on luck. Not that I have anything against luck. It's just when I'm on a case, I find most of my luck is bad.

I look at Carol. "Have you picked up any thoughts that might be from Saturn?" I ask.

Carol takes a deep breath and then another. She closes her eyes. Another deep breath. She opens her eyes. "No," she says softly. "Though it's really hard to filter out all the ambient human thoughts."

"Dogs hear things differently than humans, right?" I say to HARV.

HARV nods. "Yes, they can detect a far greater range of sounds."

I figure I have a couple of options. We can take advantage of Saturn being a dog and slightly psionic. We can let him know Merinda is worried about him and we are looking for him.

"OK," I tell HARV and Carol. "Let's not leave this to chance. We'll draw Saturn to us…"

"That would be an excellent idea," HARV says. "As long as you mean the dog, not the planet." He has a wry smile on his face.

"Yes, of course I mean the dog."

HARV shakes his head. "I can never be sure with you. You have taken many blows to the cranium."

Behind HARV, I see Carol snickering. Yep, my team loves me.

"Here's the plan," I say pointing to HARV. "Broadcast—in a frequency only dogs can hear—that today, right outside the museum in the park, is an exhibit of the world's biggest fire hydrant."

I point to Carol. "You broadcast psionically the same message. Maybe toss in that vendors will be giving away dog treats."

As we head toward the museum, HARV says, "Do you really think this will work?"

I shrug. "It can't hurt."

"Unless Saturn gets angry that there is no giant fire hydrant and no dog treats and bites you in the butt," HARV snickers.

"Yeah, I'll have you project a giant holographic fire hydrant. That should make him happy enough to get a couple of tail wags." I look at Carol. "Plus, change the dog treats to belly rubs."

We walk for a few more minutes, all the while keeping our eyes—or simulated eyes—peeled, looking for Saturn. We don't spot him, but the park's museum soon comes into view. I know the museum here is well over a hundred years old, but they renovate it every few decades. It's a three-level copper building that is meant to be modern and yet ordinary, as if it just sprung up naturally among all the trees in the park. An observation tower shaped like an upside-down pyramid accents the building. The tower was meant to look all New Wavy when it was first added onto the building, and thanks to today's eclectic tastes in design, it still looks fairly futuristic.

The quad leading to the museum has many sculptures dotting its landscape. We can take advantage of this.

"OK, HARV," I say, pointing to an open spot between sculptures of a giant apple and a rainbow. "That looks like a good place to project our world's biggest fire hydrant."

HARV nods in agreement.

A second later, a man-size orange and red fire hydrant appears in what was the open space. I know it's only the image of a fire hydrant, but it looks perfectly solid.

HARV smiles and puffs out his chest. "The quality is so fine due to my new patented solid light technology."

"Good for you," I say, patting him on the shoulder. I turn to Carol. "Are you broadcasting a 'come here' message?"

"Yes," Carol answers.

"If this doesn't draw him out, he's not in this park," I say.

"It's going to work," Carol tells me, putting her hand to her forehead. "I can sense an intelligence that's not human coming toward us." Carol points toward some bushes that outline the quad area.

Sure enough, a long furry nose pops out from the bushes. A golden-brown collie sticks his entire head out and sniffs around. The dog darts out from the protection of the bushes and scampers toward us. Saturn bounds across the field with the unbridled joy that only a dog can muster.

I smile. It's nice when a case works out.

Suddenly, maybe twenty meters from us, Saturn drops to the ground, stopping dead in his tracks. My keen PI eye spots a tranq needle jutting out of his neck.

A bot hovers above him. "Unlicensed canine spotted and stopped." A net pops out from the bot and telescopes toward the now out-cold Saturn. "Offending animal to be detained."

"You smiled too soon," HARV tells me. "You managed to get Saturn captured by a DCB—a dogcatcher bot."

"Yeah, he's not captured yet," I growl.

I watch the net from the dogcatcher bot move closer and closer to Saturn.

"I didn't get this close to be stopped by some two-bit bot," I snarl.

"Zach, DCBs have way more than two-bit processors. While they are not nearly as advanced as say, I am, they still need the processing power to identify a dog, determine if it is a stray, and then apprehend it." HARV notices me glaring at him. "Oh, perhaps you are referring to the price of the bot using an antiquated term? In that, I must inform you that DCBs cost far more than two bits—" HARV's eyes start to flash. "In fact, they cost twenty thousand credits." HARV studies me for a nanosecond. "Therefore, if you are planning to blow away the bot, the fine will be twenty thousand credits for the new bot, plus another twenty-five thousand credits for discharging your weapon in public without cause." HARV points a finger at me. "I'm sure you are aware that even licensed PIs are not allowed to do that." HARV puts his hands on his hips and lifts his head in thought. "Still, Merinda is paying you two hundred thousand credits for finding Saturn. So you would still turn a profit despite the charges."

I scratch my chin. "Yeah, but those fees are obscene. This is a matter of principle. What are our chances of reasoning with the dogcatcher bot and getting it to give us Saturn?"

"The dog or the planet?" HARV asks.

"The dog." I sigh.

"You would have just as much chance as getting the planet from the DCB. DCBs are very single-minded. Once they capture a dog, they will only release it to its owner, after he or she pays a twenty thousand credit fine." HARV's eyes blink red. "Plus there would be a twenty-five thousand credit processing fee."

"Doesn't that seem a bit excessive?" I ask.

HARV nods. "Apparently, they do not want people to let their dogs roam free and, well, do what dogs do all over town. Frisco prides itself on cleanliness."

"Plus, it is kind of irresponsible to let your dog roam free," Carol adds.

I take a deep breath and think about my options. Saturn is now in the dogcatcher bot's net, so I don't have a lot of time. I need to blow the bot away, but in a quiet way that won't attract attention. "HARV, are dogcatcher bots EMP-proof?"

"Actually, no," HARV tells me. "Interesting enough, the New Frisco City Council did debate the issue five years ago but considered it to be too cost inefficient, even in a city with Zachary Nixon Johnson." HARV smiles at me. "How nice that they recognize you."

I reach down into my left ankle holster and pull out my backup weapon: GUS. GUS looks harmless enough, like a long white tube. GUS is actually one of the most powerful weapons on Earth. I don't like to use him much because, well, he has a personality.

As soon as my hand touches GUS, he glows into life.

"GUS, reporting and ready for action, Mr. Johnson, sir!" he shouts. "How are we saving the world today?"

I aim GUS at the dogcatcher bot. "You're going to fire an electromagnetic pulse at that DCB."

"That doesn't sound very sporting," GUS says.

Having a weapon with a personality can be a real pain in the behind. I always have to convince GUS that he is being used properly.

"GUS, if we don't do this, a poor, innocent dog that doesn't know our laws will be put in doggy prison. Who knows what could happen to him there?"

GUS hums for a second. It's the theme from Jeopardy.

"Acknowledged," GUS says. "EMP fired."

The dogcatcher bot drops from the sky. Carol and I rush over to Saturn. As I remove the net from Saturn, Carol sends out soothing mental messages to the crowd of onlookers to make sure they don't question my actions.

Saturn looks up at me and grins. He is groggy, but conscious. "Nice job, Mr. Johnson," he thinks to me. "You passed our test. We have a problem. One of her staff wants to kill Merinda. We need you to find out which one."

5

The good news is HARV, Carol, and I have found Saturn and are now walking him back to Merinda, his *owner* or *boss* or *buddy* or whatever. The bad—or at least, interesting—news is it appears Saturn's running away was a ploy to get us alone with the dog.

"Did I hear you correctly?" I think to Saturn.

"If you heard that somebody wants to kill my friend Merinda, then yes," Saturn thinks to me.

"This is different," Carol thinks to both of us.

"What? What? What?" HARV complains in my brain. "I can't hear anything from Saturn, only you two…"

"Sorry, HARV, we'll fill you in when we get more info," I say. I turn my attention back to Saturn. "So what makes you think somebody wants to kill Merinda?"

Saturn looks up at me from Carol's arms. "On our trip here, as we were arriving, I picked up a thought—a very angry thought: I am going to kill Merinda."

"Are you sure?" I ask. "That's a pretty serious allegation."

"Of course I'm sure!" Saturn thinks and whimpers. "I'm very attuned to people's thoughts."

"Then how come you can't identify the thinker?" I prompt.

Saturn shakes his head and pants a little. I assume that's his sign of frustration. It appears I have a knack for frustrating all sorts of mammals. "Mr. Johnson, as I am sure you have noticed, I am a dog. While I am a very advanced dog, one who hardly ever sniffs a butt, I still have trouble identifying or pinpointing stray thoughts from other species…"

"It is hard," Carol chimes in,. She pets him. Saturn starts wagging his tail.

"Why would anybody want to harm Merinda?" I ask.

"Humans can be quite petty and mean," Saturn thinks to me.

"While I still can't pick up Saturn's thoughts, I can read yours clearly," HARV says. "It is my understanding that many on Mars do not want Mars to improve their relationship with Earth."

"HARV, I'm relaying your thoughts to Saturn," Carol thinks to all of us.

"The electronic being is right. Many on Mars want things to stay exactly how they are. They look at Earth as petty and corrupt, and would do anything to stop us from having anything to do with you," Saturn thinks.

I assume Carol relays those thoughts to HARV while I process the information. I can certainly believe that some Martians wouldn't want to increase their ties to Earth. Mars Colony is officially only twenty-three years old, yet it prides itself on its independence. Of course, even though it is officially only twenty-three years old, I know the colony has been around longer, as the Gladians have been keeping human clones on Mars for well over fifty years. The official Gladian line is that they were helping out Earth by keeping backup humans around, just in case. So you can't blame Martians for being a little leery.

"How many others were on the flight here with you besides Merinda and Alicia?" I ask.

"There were three others: Maxxx, who is Merinda's bodyguard; Tezza, her PR person; and HAL50, her consultant…" HARV says.

"No pilot on the ship?" I ask.

"No pilot needed," HARV says. "The ship is piloted by the SRIP, a smart robot intelligent pilot system."

"OK, are the others still looking for you?" I ask Saturn.

"Yes."

"OK, HARV. Contact Merinda and let her know we have Saturn, but tell her not to tell the others, even Alicia."

"Check, boss."

It seems obvious to me that somebody aboard that ship doesn't want Mars and Earth to have closer ties. "I need to learn more about each of the people traveling with Merinda."

"HAL50 is actually an android with a human brain," HARV tells me.

"Well then, I need to learn more about all the people and near humans traveling with Merinda. When is Merinda supposed to meet with the World Council?" I ask.

"Tomorrow at noon," HARV tells me.

"OK, get me as much info on the crew as you can!"

"Zach, I'm having trouble gathering information on Maxxx, Tezza, Alicia, and HAL50. Being Martians, we don't have much data on them," HARV informs me.

"Talk to the intelligent ship. I am sure it has some data."

"I have, and the SRIP ship says, and I quote, 'Sorry. No go, Earthling,'" HARV answers.

"That's not helpful," I say.

"It's insulting," HARV says. "I consider myself being above planetary boundaries."

"OK, HARV, talk to Merinda and see if she can get SRIP to open up." Looking at Saturn, I say, "What can you tell me about Merinda's shipmates?"

"Well—as a dog, you know—I pretty much trust everybody."

"Yeah, but any of them that you just want to bite now and then?" I probe.

"Mr. Johnson, I may be an animal, but I'm not an animal."

"OK then, just give me your initial impressions."

Saturn looks up at me. "Well, I'll give you my feedback, but please remember I am biased, being a dog and all. I can't imagine Maxxx, Tezza, and Alicia ever hurting Merinda. They have all been with her for as long as I can remember, and they are very loyal—almost as loyal as I am. Of course, that being said, they will do whatever they feel is necessary to help Mars thrive."

"OK then, what about the robot with the human brain?"

"HAL50 is hard to read. He is not a true citizen of Mars. He is an Earth expatriate. He said he never felt comfortable on Earth."

"HARV and Carol, are you getting all this?" I think to them.

"Yes, Carol is relaying the information to me. It's a weird, but functional, way to communicate. I am looking up information on HAL50 now." HARV informs me.

"Halt, Zachary Nixon Johnson!" I hear coming from above us.

Looking up, I see three golden metal cylinders with big, red, pulsating sensors on top. They are dropping toward us. I recognize these cylinders as World Council drones.

"How in the DOS does the Would Council know we are here, and why would they care?" I mumble.

"I've been mentally talking with my grandma, your future mother-in-law, Councilwoman Helena Gevada," Carol says. That explains why she's been so quiet. "I thought they might know if anybody on Earth was less than thrilled by Earth and Mars improving their relationships. Please don't be angry."

I lean over and give her a little hug. Looking her in the eyes, I tell her, "How could I be mad? That's actually good PI work."

Of course, the drones droned on. "Zachary Nixon Johnson, your presence is immediately required."

I look up at the drones, which are now mere meters from us. Holding up a finger and pointing at Saturn, I say, "I actually want to talk to the World Council myself. But first, I need to return this poor dog to his owner. I can be at World Council HQ in an hour, two tops."

The three drones lock their laser sights on me. Three red dots appear on the middle of my body. I raise my hands slowly.

"It appears the World Council wants to see you now," HARV tells me.

"Yeah, typical politicians. It takes them forever to get anything done, yet they think their time is so much more valuable than ours," I mutter to HARV and Carol. Turning to the floating drones, I remind them, "My future mother-in-law, Helena, is the one who sent you. There is no way she would let you kill me. Electra—my girlfriend and Helena's daughter—would be *way* upset."

"We are the latest in drone technology. We are equipped with the PAIN weapons system," one of the drones says to me, like I'm supposed to know what that means.

HARV leans in to me and for some reason whispers, "It stands for 'person's attitude instant neutralizer.' It causes a subject to experience the worst pain in his or her life without actually killing the person. It's quite nifty and a great acroynm."

Now Carol leans in to me. "Now, that is something my grandma, Helena, would do to you."

I don't doubt Carol on that one. Helena has made it clear that while she does tolerate me (after all, I have saved the world a few times), she doesn't think I am nearly good enough for her little girl. Thing is, there has been a threat to Merinda's life. I need to get to the bottom of that before it's too late.

"HARV, how much do these bots cost?" I ask mentally.

"Each drone costs ten million credits."

"That seems pretty pricey."

"Agreed. The drones should only cost five million credits, but the WC pays extra for the gold chrome. They justify that by saying tax payers expect them to have the best."

OK, so it would be expensive to destroy the drones, plus it probably wouldn't be a great career move getting the World Council angry at me, especially since my future mother-in-law is on the council. I need a way to get out of this peacefully, but still get my way. I look over at Saturn sitting contentedly in Carol's arms. That's my key to getting out of this. Trick is, I can't move too quickly without the drones activating the PAIN system.

"Carol, float Saturn over to me," I think.

Carol releases her hold on Saturn, and he glides over to me. I take Saturn in my arms and show him to the drones.

"Shoot me now, while I'm holding a cute dog from Mars in my arms, and you will cause quite the media uproar," I inform the drones.

The drones' red lights start blinking.

"You have an incoming message from esteemed Councilwoman Helena Gevada. Will you accept it?" the three drones drone in unison.

"Ah, sure."

The holographic image of my future mother-in-law appears in front of me, projected from the middle drone. Helena is a strong, confident woman, much like her daughter. In fact, she is so confident, she has no problem letting her hair grow gray. That's something you don't see much of these days.

"Hello, Zach," she says.

"Helena," I say.

"Hi, Abuela," Carol says with a wave.

"Zach," Helena tells me. "I may have been a bit too forceful trying to convince you to come see me first. But I really do feel it will be in your best interest to see me before you make another move."

weigh Helena's words. I need to get Saturn back to Merinda, but I also figure it is in my best interest to at least hear Helena out.

"I'll be there ASAP," I tell Helena.

"Very well," she says with a smile. "My drones will bring you in." Before I have a chance to reply, she pushes a button and her holographic image disappears.

The drones levitate over to me. "Are you ready, Mr. Johnson?" they ask.

Holding up a finger, I tell them, "One minute, please." I turn to Carol and hand her Saturn. "Here, take Saturn to Merinda and stay by her side. Tell her not to call back any of her people yet. I don't want them alone with her until I get back there."

"Got it," Carol says, taking Saturn into her arms.

"I thank you for this," Saturn thinks to me.

I pet him on the head. "Don't thank me until I figure out who's behind all this." Looking up at the drones, I say, "OK, drones, I'm ready to roll."

The drones just hover there.

"That means he's ready to go," HARV tells them.

The middle drone flies directly over me. "This won't hurt a bit," it reassures me. A net shoots out of the drone's bottom part. The net lands on top of me, engulfing me.

"Sweet, a nano net," HARV says as the drone lifts me up into the air.

"Well, this is kind of undignified," I groan.

"Yeah, but it's still not the worst way you've ever traveled," HARV tells me.

Trying to get my mind off of being dragged through the air in a drone's net, I turn my attention back to the case.

"HARV, I need you to coax the intelligent ship SRIP a bit more. See if we can get any clues."

"I tried that once before, and he was less than responsive."

"Then be charming, HARV. Surely you can be charming."

"Zach, I am not a human. Therefore, I have no ego for you to stroke, but I will try."

We float through the air for a few more minutes. The shiny ivory tower that is the World Council building comes into view.

"Any luck, HARV?"

"Zach, I am a highly sophisticated cognitive processor. I do not need luck."

"Any progress?"

Silence.

"SRIP insists he is doing lots of really important work preparing for his flight back to Mars. He has the lives of his passengers to take into account first."

"So no," I think back.

"Wipe that smug smile off your face, Zach. I will get through to him."

We are over the roof of the World Council building, and the drones have started their descent. At least the two drones beside us have. The one carrying me actually starts rising.

"Ah, what gives, drone?" I ask.

"I am going to a greater height," the drone tells me.

"Yeah, I see that, but why?"

"I want to reach a greater altitude to assure your death when I crash myself to the ground."

OK, kinda sorry I asked that.

"See, this is why you're the last freelance PI on Earth," HARV tells me.

As the drone lifts me higher and higher, I make an attempt to reason with it. I pop my gun into my hand and wave it in front of the drone's sensor.

"Land now, or I blow you away," I say in my best tough-guy growl.

"Sir, I am planning on destroying myself as well as you, so your threat is truly an empty one. Either way you will die, and my mission will be accomplished."

"It's got you there," HARV tells me.

"HARV—you still in communication with the other drones?"

"Yes, of course."

Using my right hand, I reach into my left-leg holster and pull out my good old-fashioned emergency knife. There are times when simple is best. Holding the top of the net and my gun with my left hand, I use the knife in my right hand to start cutting through the bottom netting.

"You are lucky the World Council cut corners and skimped on the nano netting for these drones. They were more concerned about their looks and cost than function," HARV tells me.

"Well, it usually doesn't make a lot of sense to cut yourself out of a net from two hundred meters in the air," I say.

"Good point." HARV agrees. "Zach, not to state the obvious, but the fall from this height will still kill you, even with your body armor. So I am assuming you have some sort of plan."

"Yeah, as soon as I cut myself loose and start to fall, I want one of the other drones to catch me with its net and then guide me gently to the ground," I say, cutting away.

"Not exactly the best plan," HARV notes.

"Do you have another, HARV?"

There's a slight silence and then HARV concedes, "Continue to cut away."

"OK, HARV, the timing is going to have to be perfect here," I say, preparing to separate myself from the drone.

"Zach, I feel I must warn you the drones are not programmed to net falling targets. Running, yes. Falling, no."

"Falling is just vertical running," I note. "Make the adjustments…" I think a moment more. "Oh, and make sure my bullet hits this drone. Can you do all that?"

"Doesn't really matter if I can or can't, since you're so committed to this plan," HARV tells me.

I cut out the bottom of the net and release my grip on the top, beginning my fall to the ground.

I let myself free fall for a second or three and then fire my gun. There's nothing left for me to do except fall and hope this plan works.

Plummeting to the ground, I hear an explosion above me. I take that as a sign I have taken out the drone that wants to kill me. The ground is looming closer and closer. I feel something wrap around me. My descent slows. Something else wraps around me. My descent stops. I find myself engulfed in two nets, dangling a meter above the roof of the World Council building as drone debris litters the ground all around me.

"You're welcome," HARV says. "I had both drones net you to compensate for your momentum."

My future mother-in-law, senior World Council member Helena Gevada, bursts through the roof door, followed by her two personal-guard bots.

"Zachary, what are you doing destroying and misusing World Council property?" she demands.

7

"I repeat, Zachary, why did you destroy and reprogram World Council property?" Helena, demands as I dangle above her.

"Remember, don't be snarky," HARV says in my head. "Helena is a powerful woman and Electra's mom."

"I was bored. So for kicks I decided to destroy one of your drones and then free fall from it so your other two drones could catch me. I figured I'd bring some excitement to their boring drone existence," I tell her.

HARV sighes.

Helena points to the top of the nets keeping me suspended in midair. "Cut him down," she orders her guard bots.

One of the bots extends a clawlike arm toward the net. The bot clips the net. I fall to the ground face first.

"Thanks," I groan. "Of course, I would prefer you didn't have your drones try to kill me in the first place."

Helena offers me her hand to help me back to my feet. "Please, Zach, senior World Council members only get so many sanctioned kills. I wouldn't waste one of mine on you."

Getting to my feet, I look her in the eyes. "That being said, somebody wants me dead."

"Zach, lots of people want you dead, but this isn't about you," Helena tells me.

"She has a very valid point," HARV chimes in.

"I mean, somebody *new* wants me dead now that I am on the Merinda case."

Helena points to the door that leads off the roof. "Now enough of this tomfoolery with drones. Let's go to my office where we can talk in private."

Helena leads me through the ornate halls of the World Council's headquarters. Looking down at the marble floors, I say, "You certainly didn't skimp when it came to this building."

"We on the council make important life- and world-changing decisions all the time. It is important that we are comfortable. Studies show that comfortable people make better decisions," Helena says.

"She's right," HARV agrees.

I glare at him.

I decide to walk the rest of the way in silence. After a few minutes, Helena opens the door to her office. The office is more spacious than my house. The wooden desk that dominates the middle of the room is larger than a city hover bus and seems to have been carved out of a redwood tree.

"Nice place," I say.

"Zach, I am one of the most popular politician in decades. My approval rating is almost over twenty-five percent," Helena says far more proudly than she should. "I deserve this office."

Helena sits behind her desk and motions for me to sit across from her. I do. She runs her hand over a sensor on the desk. A dome lowers from the cathedral ceiling.

"So we can truly talk in private," Helena says as the dome covers us.

Helena sits there with her back arched until the dome locks in place. Then, "Zach, I consider this meeting with Merinda very important. Building a relationship between Mars and Earth would be beneficial to both our worlds. But Zach, I am much more open-minded and freethinking than my colleagues, hence my mass popularity and why—"

"Get to the point, please, Helena."

Helena locks eyes with me. "If there was an attempt on Merinda's life, it might have been sponsored by somebody here. I know a few council members who want to keep things status quo between Earth and Mars."

"Can you tell me which of your cronies you suspect?" I ask. I lean toward Helena. "I repeat, will you rat out your fellow council member or members? Who would want to see Merinda dead? How could they gain by hurting the Earth-Mars relationship?"

Helena bends over the desk, grabs my collar, and pulls me toward her quite violently. "Zach! How dare you ask me that!"

I keep calm. Locking my eyes on her, I raise a finger and say, "First, you're the one who brought this up. I don't have a lot of time to fool around, so yeah, I dare ask you." I raise a second finger and tell her, "Second, while I don't hit ladies, unless of course they are trained assassins and trying to kill me, I am not against shocking you."

Helena releases my collar and lets me drop to the chair. She sits back and smiles. "Just messing with you, my boy. I want to see what the man my daughter plans to marry is made of." Helena crosses her arms and looks at me smugly. "Not to throw mud, but I totally suspect it's Sexy Sprockets."

I worked with Sexy a couple of times back in the day when she was a teen-age rock star, before old age (turning twenty) forced her to go into politics. "Come on, Helena. Sexy is vapid and shallow, but she's not a killer."

"She's also the one politician in the world more popular than Helena," HARV notes.

Helena leans back deeper in her chair. "She spent a lot of years in the music industry. You don't get more diabolical than music execs. Surely, some of that must have rubbed off on her."

I shrug. "So what would Sexy gain from disrupting the Earth-Mars relationship?"

Helena returns my shrug with one of her own. "One of Sexy's biggest backers is HyperUltraMaxMart. It would lose profit if Earth were suddenly flooded with handmade products from Mars."

"That is true," HARV tells me in my head.

"Well first, I can't imagine HyperUltraMaxMart would lose *that* much profit. And second, I'm pretty sure it backs all you politicians."

"That is also true," HARV says in my head. "This year alone, Helena has received over a million credits from HUMM."

Helena smirks. "Zach, what is this obsession you have with counting?"

"Just answer the question, Helena."

She sighs. "Yes, HUMM does contribute to my causes, but I'm not the one who started the Earth First Act. That is being championed by Sexy and

Councilman Sam Storm. If that bill passes, all products not made on Earth will be taxed three hundred percent."

"I'm sure you are familiar with Sam Storm. Before his political career, he was a pitcher for the Mexico City Padres," HARV says.

"I actually forgot all about Sam Storm since he retired from baseball," I say.

"He's not one of the more outspoken World Council members," Helena says. "But that doesn't make him or Sexy any less calculating." She pushes a button on her desk. The dome rises up off of us.

At that moment, Sexy Sprockets comes bursting into Helena's office. I swear her blond hair is longer than her red miniskirt and pink halter. Sexy stands there, arms crossed, stiletto boots tapping furiously on the ground. "Helena, Zachster, I demand to know why you are talking about me."

Helena holds open her palms to Sexy in a calming gesture. "Sexy, whatever makes you believe we were talking about you?"

Sexy's face turns red, matching her skirt. "Can the crap, Helena. Remember, I'm a psi with years in the music business. I can tell whenever somebody is saying bad things about me." Sexy makes a fist and shakes it at us. "Now I demand to know what the DOS is going on here! I repeat, Zachy, I demand to know what the WTFing DOS you are doing here talking about me!" Sexy shouts.

Years of being a PI have taught me you can learn a lot about a person watching how he or she reacts to a nasty truth.

"I'll tell you, as long as you promise never to call me *Zachy* again."

"Deal, Zach-attack," Sexy says.

"Wait, what?" Helena says, grabbing my arm.

"She deserves to know," I say, without looking back at Helena.

Looking directly at Sexy, I tell her, "There was a threat on Merinda-1616's life." Yes, it's a small spinning of the truth, but a spinning that fits my need. "Talking to Helena here, she thinks you might have a thing against Mars and Merinda. After all, you are one of the sponsors of the Earth First Act."

"What?" Sexy screams, her face now turning redder than her miniskirt. "How could you, b——!"

Sexy leaps at Helena, grabs her, and they start rolling on the ground, exchanging physical and mental blows.

"You tone-deaf bimbo. I'll show you what pain really is!"

"You're just jealous of my youth and red-hot body!"

"Oh please, why would I be jealous of a dumb, tone-deaf bimbo with no taste or style?"

"Take that back! I have lots of style!"

"HARV, are you recording this? It could come in handy in the future."

"Of course. Have you gotten what you need yet? Not to be a pest, but we really should be getting back to Merinda and Carol soon. After all, Merinda can't keep her people looking much longer for a dog that we already found."

"Yeah, Sexy has nothing to do with this. I saw her made-for-HV special, *Love Sucks at the Soul*. She's not nearly a good enough actress to pull off this kind of fake anger."

"I concur. I've run voice analyses on both ladies, and they seem to be telling the truth."

"OK, ladies, that's enough!" I shout.

I walk over to the two, who are still rolling on the floor pounding each other. Bending down, I pull Sexy off of Helena. Helena kicks at Sexy from the floor, but I block her kick. "That would have been a low blow, even for a politician," I scold.

I offer my hand to Helena. She accepts it, and I pull her to her feet.

"I'm pretty certain neither of you has anything to do with the threat against Merinda," I tell them. "Now I just need to talk to your fellow council person, Sam Storm, just to gauge if he has anything to do with this."

"Impossible," Helena tells me. "He's on a top-secret fact-finding tour."

Sexy nods. "Yep, we can't just tell you where one of us really important people is."

"Well, it's nice to know that you two can at least agree on something."

"We also agree that World Council members are vastly underpaid," Sexy says proudly.

"You got that right, sister," Helena says, fist raised.

Sexy turns to Helena. "You can't believe how much more lucrative it was being a teen pop-rock idol slash goddess."

"Oh, I can believe it!"

I cough. "Ah, ladies. I'm trying to prevent a murder here. So it would really help if you helped me."

The two ladies cross their arms and clamp their mouths shut. You didn't have to be a PI to know they weren't going to tell me anything.

"Look, ladies, I know you are busy politicians," I say, putting air quotes around the word *busy*. "But I need to question Sam Storm—see if he might be involved in this."

The two stare at me, hands on hips.

"Zachy, you know we can't do that," Sexy says. "It would be bad form."

Helena nods. "For one of the few times in my career, I agree with Sexy."

"In that case, you ladies leave me no choice." I turn my wrist communicator toward them. "HARV, play the video."

The holographic image of Helena and Sexy rolling on the floor trading blows appears.

"I look good on top," Sexy says with a smile.

"You two don't want this to go public, do you?" I say.

Sexy shrugs. "Oh, Zach-man, my fans—I mean voters…I mean constituents—love me no matter what I do. If anything, they will just complain we weren't doing it in mud."

"She's got you there," HARV whispers to me.

I set my sights on Helena, zeroing in on her. I ask, "What about you? Wasn't your last slogan 'The most distinguished politician in the worlds'?"

Helena sighs. "Sam is stepping down from politics at the end of the month. He's tired of all the red tape. But he wants to go out with a bang, so he's on the moon trying to work out a new trade deal with them."

"But why sponsor the Earth First Act, then?" I ask. "Products from the moon would be heavily taxed."

"Sam is trying to work out a deal where Earth would annex the moon and the moon would become part of Earth," Helena says.

"That's crazy!" I say.

Sexy nods. "Yep, Zachy-poo, I agree."

Helena holds her ground. "Obviously, for those on the moon, their fierce love of independence makes it a difficult task to accomplish, yet it would certainly be a great start to his new career in the private sector. It's a win for everybody."

"Everybody except Mars," I point out.

Helena shakes her head. "It sets a precedent for them to become part of Earth, too."

OK, this wasn't exactly what I was expecting, but this could be a good break. I have dealt with the people of the moon on a number of occasions. I have one very good contact there: Elena Sputnik. Elena is a high-level psi whom I have fought against and with. She is fiercely loyal to the moon, where she is on its ruling council. She would certainly know what Sam Storm is up to there.

"HARV, make contact with Elena. Tell her I need to see her ASAP."

"Done, Zach."

"Let me know when you have a response, HARV."

A bright, human-size ball of energy appears in the middle of the room.

HARV points at the crackling ball. "I think her response is coming."

The ball of energy fizzes away. There stands Elena Sputnik in all her glory: sparkling-green eyes; long, blue hair; a smooth, peach complexion—all somehow perfectly complemented by a purple dress and knee-high purple boots.

"You called?" Elena says.

Sexy and Helena are quick to react.

"Elena, baby, I so love those boots, but this is so uncool coming in unannounced!" Sexy scolds.

"This is a brazen breach of protocol!" Helena shouts at her.

Elena points at the two lady politicians. "Mute and pause!" she orders.

The two freeze in place.

Elena blows on her index finger and then lowers it. "I love doing that," she giggles. "Now, Zach, you called?"

I look at the two frozen politicians. I turn to Elena and decide to just get to the point. "Elena, I need you to tell me what you know about Sam Storm."

She shrugs. "He's a boring windbag who loves the sound of his own voice."

"Yeah, he's a politician, so that goes without saying. I need to know how his negotiations with the moon are going," I prompt.

Elena laughs and waves at me with a dismissive hand. "Oh, silly Zachary. There were no negotiations. Yes, Storm did come to us about a month ago, but we totally shot down his agenda. We on the moon have no love for Mars, but we certainly aren't going to strike an exclusive deal with Earth. We don't exactly trust you guys, either. Many of you are jealous that our entire female population and some of our male population are psis."

"Not jealous, more like leery," I tell her. "But that's not the point here. The point is you turned down Sam Storm."

"Yes, of course," Elena says.

"HARV, get me more background information on Storm—his education, any business deals he's made," I think. Pointing to Helena and Sexy, I ask Elena, "Will you please unpause them?"

"But I like 'em that way," Elena pouts. "They are so peaceful and quiet."

"Elena, please."

Elena nods, and Sexy and Helena unfreeze.

"Zach, I have Storm's background. As you are aware, he was a pitcher. But in college he was actually a good student. He majored in biocomputing and got an MBA. After his career in baseball, he started a successful computer start-up company, MicroMax. It made implantable bionics that were totally undetectable by normal bioscans…Interestingly enough, he sold the technology to the World Council right before he became a member."

OK, that was something I didn't realize about Sam Storm. I am not sure how that all fits into this, at least not yet.

I turn to the now-unpaused Sexy and Helena. "Did you two know Storm's deal with the moon was a no go?"

They both shake their heads. "Ah, no," Sexy tells me.

"He e-mailed me just a day ago that the deal was dragging on," Helena says.

"That's confirmed," HARV tells me.

"Can you trace that e-mail?" I ask HARV.

"Yes, it's actually coming from a server on the moon from the No Seasons Hotel there."

Crossing my arms, I look to Elena and say, "So you're sure? Storm's deal with the moon fell through?"

"Yes, of course, Zachary."

"Then why is he sending e-mails from the moon?"

Elena takes a slight step backward. "Zachary..." She puts her hand over her heart. "I had no idea he was still on the moon. Trust me, Zachary."

I turn my attention to Helena and Sexy. "Do you ladies have any idea why Storm would stay on the moon?"

"He's probably too ashamed to come back," Sexy suggests.

"Please, he's a politician. He knows no shame," I tell her.

"Maybe he's hoping to get another shot at the Moon Council?" Helena suggests. "He is a persistent fellow."

I hear Carol in my mind. "Zach, Merinda's people are getting antsy. We need you back here."

Carol must be very anxious to remotely project a message into my brain. Still, there's something about this Sam Storm business that isn't sitting right with me...but that could be unrelated.

"Zach, you really need to get back here," Carol psionically shouts into my brain. "Merinda's staff are getting anxious to come back."

Carol is right. It is time to return to Merinda. I need to figure out—and face—whichever of her travel mates from Mars is an immediate threat. But that doesn't mean I can't multitask somewhat.

I turn to Helena and Sexy and give them a polite bow, playing up to their egos a bit. "I appreciate your help, ladies. If you hear from Sam Storm, I would also appreciate it if you would let me know. He is a person of interest to me. After all, I believe a trade agreement between Earth and Mars will benefit all."

Helena and Sexy exchange quick glances with each other.

"We will take that under advisement," Helena says.

"Yeppers," Sexy says.

Elena puts her hands on her hips and leans in to me. "How does a Mars-Earth agreement help the moon?"

"It shows the people of the moon that you are strong and don't need ties to Earth to survive," I say.

"Good one," HARV tells me.

Elena smiles. "There is a large amount of bio waste in that, but some of it also rings true. Zach, you could have a future in politics."

"Now that's a scary thought," I tell her.

Out of the corner of my eye, I see Helena nodding in agreement.

"Elena, could you port me back to the Kardasian Towers?" I ask. Yeah, I hate porting, but I've been keeping Merinda waiting too long. A good PI puts his client's needs in front of his own fears.

"Gladly," Elena says. She moves forward, putting her arms around me.

"Do you have to hug me in front of my future mother-in-law?" I ask.

Elena just smiles. She pushes a button on her belt. The next thing I know, we are standing in the lobby of the KT hotel. Elena releases me from her hug and takes a step back.

"Is there anything else I can help you with?"

"Actually, there is," I say.

Elena sighs. "You know, Zach, I was just being polite when I asked that."

Putting a hand on her shoulder and looking her in the eyes, I say, "But surely you are at least somewhat interested in what Sam Storm is doing on the moon, if he really is on the moon."

Elena dips her head a little and looks away from me. "So you want me to see if Stone is really on the moon and what he might be up to."

"That would be ideal. After all, you don't want Earth politicians hanging out on the moon. That would just be bad." I tell her.

Elena nods. "Agreed." She touches a button on her belt and disappears in a flash of energy.

"Well, that went as well as can be expected," I tell HARV.

HARV appears next to me, projecting himself from my wrist P-Pod. "Yes, it did. Now let's hope your luck holds with our next interview."

"Ah, HARV, what does that mean?"

"I've taken the liberty of contacting Twoa Thompson," HARV informs me.

Twoa Thompson is one of the Thompson Quads, four women who are genetically engineered to shear perfection. The three remaining Quads are the epitome of humankind, but they all come with super quirks, also. Twoa, for her part, considers herself to be a superhero called Justice Babe. She flies around town in a skimpy costume beating the pulp out of evildoers.

"Why, HARV? Why?"

"Zach, for all her quirks, Twoa is one of the richest women in the world. She is a major stockholder in HyperUltraMaxMart. It sells more goods than any company on Earth. It is possible they would be less than pleased about Earth getting goods from Mars."

Before I can respond to HARV, I hear, "Zachary Nixon Johnson, I am so glad you called for my aid!"

I turn and see Twoa Thompson in all her super glory flying toward me.

Twoa grabs me, locking me in a giant bear hug. "So, fellow fighter of evil, how can I help?"

"I probably should tell you that I didn't tell Twoa why you wanted to see her," HARV whispers in my mind.

8

"So, Zach, I repeat—why did your hologram summon me?" Twoa asks, releasing her grip and letting me drop to the ground.

"Ah, well, I won't beat around the bush. I understand you own a nice portion of HUMM," I say slowly.

Twoa nods. "Yes, superhero work doesn't pay well, especially since I wreck so many buildings and hovers and stuff. It's nice to have the income rolling and rolling."

"I assume you are aware of the impending talks between Earth and Mars," I say.

Twoa locks her gaze on me. "Yes, of course." I swear I see a bit of steam coming out of her ears, and her face turns slightly redder. "I don't think I'm going to like where you are going with this."

"Well, you have to admit, HUMM would lose some profits if Earth started importing products from Mars."

Twoa moves forward, faster than my eyes can detect. She grabs me, and the next thing I know, I'm flying upward toward the ceiling of the hotel.

"You really do have a way with people," HARV says in my head. "I think you should listen to my suggestion to switch colognes. It may not help, but it couldn't hurt."

I brace for impact. I'm pretty sure this is going to hurt, but nothing my body underarmor can't handle.

I stop suddenly, mere centimeters from crashing into the ceiling. I feel myself floating gently back to the ground. Out of the corner of my eye, I see Carol exiting the elevator and entering the lobby.

"I called Carol when Twoa arrived," HARV informs me. "I thought we might need some backup."

"You have so little faith in me," I tell him, just as my feet touch back gently on the ground.

Carol comes storming over toward us, her hair rippling with energy. "Not cool, Twoa!" she shouts, pointing an accusing finger.

Twoa rolls her eyes. "You're not the only one with telekinetic powers," she says to Carol. "I was just funning Zach a bit, superhero to sidekick. I wasn't going to let him crash."

"Twoa—one, I don't call tossing me into the ceiling fun. And two, and more importantly, I am *not* your sidekick."

"Yes, if anything he is *my* sidekick," HARV chimes in.

"I'm nobody's sidekick!" I shout.

"Not with an attitude like that," Twoa tells me.

"Agreed," HARV says, with a nod toward Twoa.

"Do you want me to zap her?" Carol asks me.

It's a tempting offer. But truthfully, despite Carol's power, I'm not sure if she could take on Twoa. I shake my head. "Not yet. I need to see if I can get some information out of her willingly."

Twoa holds open her arms. "Zach, I really did come here to help."

I shoot a finger into Twoa's face. I figure if I talk fast, I might get her to give up some 411. "So what are HUMM's interests in Earth and Mars's relationship?"

Twoa puts her arm around me. I'm not sure if it's meant to be a friendly gesture, or if she wants to zap me with super pheromones. Either way, I like it.

"Zach, we at HUMM are all for opening up trade relations with Mars. In fact, we plan to negotiate with them to be the distributor of their goods here. After all, HUMM sells eighty-eight percent of all goods and 3-D printer plans on Earth, either online or in our stores, for those old-fashioned types. The way we see it, the more goods we have to offer, the better. Our studies have shown the more people buy, the more they want to buy."

"That is confirmed," HARV says.

I have to admit that HyperUltraMaxMart working with Mars would make sense. It could be a win-win for both of them.

"Do you want me to make sure she's telling the truth?" Carol asks. "Let me scan her, tió." Carol never takes her green eyes off of Twoa. "I can tell if she's telling the truth."

Twoa curls her fingers into fists and shakes them at Carol. "Just try, psi!"

I think about it for a moment, about what Twoa said about HyperUltraMegaMart actually benefiting from an Earth-Mars trade agreement. It makes sense. Stepping between Carol and Twoa, I tell Carol, "No need. I think we can trust Twoa." I say the last part loud enough so Twoa can easily hear me without resorting to super hearing.

"Of course you can trust me, Zach-boy. I am one of the good gals," Twoa exclaims, holding her hand out for me to shake.

Shaking her hand, I say, "Please don't call me *Zach-boy*. I am not a sidekick."

"Of course," Twoa says in a tone that doesn't match the words.

Twoa releases her grip on me and extends a hand to Carol. Carol eyes Twoa's hand as a snake handler would eye a cobra. Carol cautiously extends her hand to meet Twoa's. The two lock their grips and glare at each other. I watch them tighten their grips. Neither of the ladies gives any ground or hint of pain. I step in between them.

"Ah, ladies, this is no time for a mental spitting contest," I tell them.

They both turn their attention to me.

"We're ladies. We don't spit," they say at once.

They release their grips, giving each other a smile of acknowledgment.

Twoa leans toward me. "So, brave Zach, are you satisfied with my answer?"

I nod. "Yes, I am."

"If you need anything else, you know how to summon me!" Twoa shouts, for no apparent reason. She lifts her arm and flies off.

"I still think I could take her if I had to," Carol tells me.

Pointing to the elevator, I say, "Let's get to Merinda's suite. I have an idea."

"Let me guess. You need me to take Alicia out so you can talk to Merinda in private," Carol says, following me toward the elevator.

"Bingo," I say, walking into the elevator.

Carol turns to HARV. "That means yes. Right?"

HARV simply nods.

"Her mind is powerful, but I believe if I touch her, then I can lower her defenses…" Carol says.

9

We find Merinda in her bedroom, sitting on her bed. Saturn has his head contentedly in her lap. Alicia is, of course, standing vigilant by Merinda's side.

"Mr. Johnson, I am so glad you found Saturn and that you are here!" Alicia tells me anxiously. "The rest of the staff will be here soon to also personally thank you."

Carol taps Alicia on the shoulder and says, "Sleep standing for me."

Alicia's eyes shut, and her head drops.

"We need to talk alone for a moment," I tell Merinda and Saturn. "I have an idea." Moving next to Merinda, I say, "I want you to cancel your meeting with the World Council."

"Why?" she asks.

"This will delay whoever wants to harm you and give me more time to figure out which one of your staff it is."

Merinda looks at me, weighing my words carefully. "*If* I delay, what would I tell the council?"

"You need to go back to Mars for personal reasons," I tell her. "They are politicians. They will totally relate to you putting your needs in front of the needs of your people."

Merinda lowers her head. "I don't know. I so hate to let my people down…"

"Merinda, delaying your meeting with the World Council will allow me time to figure out who wants you dead."

Merinda stands there weighing my words, so I decide to add a little more heft to them.

"You getting dead isn't good for your people or the people of Earth," I toss in.

Merinda stands there for a moment in thought. Raising her arm, she types something on her wrist communicator. "I am texting the World Council and my colleagues on the Mars Council, telling them I need to delay for a week due to a personal matter."

I smile and nod. "I gotta respect a lady who puts off the World Council with a text."

Merinda looks up at me, eyes wide open. "I assured them the matter would not take longer than a week. I don't want to hurt relationships between our planets. You can solve this in a week. Correct, Zach?"

"Yes, I will solve this within the week," I say in my most reassuring voice. Pointing to Alicia, I tell Carol, "We better get rolling. Unfreeze the aide so she can get the rest of the Mars people here."

Before Carol can react, Merinda's wrist communicator starts to beep.

Looking at the communicator, Merinda says, "It's from my sister on Mars Council, Beka."

Merinda touches her communicator. The holographic image of a woman who looks like a blond (with red-and-blue streaks), fairer-skinned version of Merinda appears.

"Beka, how nice of you to call," Merinda says.

"So, sister, why are you delaying our talks with Earth?" Beka asks, eyebrow raised.

"I just had a traumatic experience. Poor Saturn went missing and was almost captured by a dogcatcher bot. Only the heroic efforts of Zachary Nixon Johnson and his staff saved us."

"I am not staff," I heard HARV mumble. "I don't get paid."

"I'm staff, but I barely get paid," Carol says.

"Big picture, team. Big picture," I tell them.

Merinda turns her communicator so Beka can see HARV, Carol, and me. We all wave politely.

"Mr. Johnson, thank you for helping my sister find our dear Saturn," Beka tells me. "Now, to repay you, I insist you come to Mars for a suitable reward."

Before I have a chance to respond, Merinda does. "What a splendid idea. We will head to Mars immediately."

Beka smiles. "I look forward to greeting you and any of your staff that you care to bring."

Beka's image fades off.

"I'm not staff," HARV says, tapping his foot angrily.

Merinda walks over to me and puts her hand on my shoulder. "Before you say anything, Zach, think about what a perfect opportunity this will be. You will have my potential killer isolated and void of any distractions."

Merinda actually makes an interesting point. On the positive side, we will be locked in a ship with a potential killer who won't be able to get away. We'd be in a controlled environment, making it easier for me to both protect Merinda and weed out her killer. Of course on the negative side, we'd be stuck in a ship with a killer. Still, no plan is perfect.

"Are you sure this is how you want to do this, Merinda? It could be dangerous," I tell her.

She takes me by the arm. "Saturn and I have faith in you. Our ship informs me it can be ready in two hours."

"Well, I guess I can be ready in two hours, then, also," I say.

Carol looks at me. "What about me, tió? Do you want me there?"

Now I have to weigh my options. On one hand, it's always useful to have a class one psi on your side. She may be able to pick up on the killer's thoughts. On the other hand, pretty much everybody now knows Carol is a psi. Having her around might force the killer to be more guarded, making him or her less likely to make a mistake or tip his or her hand.

I weigh my options with Carol carefully. It's almost always useful to have a psi on your side. Still, people from Mars—Martians—aren't quite like normal Earth humans. From what I know, most Martians have bionics. If some of these enhancements were to their brains, it could make it dicey to deal with them, especially if they could somehow detect Carol was probing their minds. I do know Carol really had to work at it to dominate Alicia.

Turning to Merinda, I ask, "How many of your people have bionics?"

Merinda smiles. "Zach, we're Martians, so we all have some sort of bionic enhancements in us. But they aren't like Earth bionics, where they are replacement parts. On Mars, we use bionics to supplement and improve. For instance, Alicia, my faithful aide, has bionic-enhanced eyes. Maxxx, my security guard, has had his arms and legs enhanced."

"OK, so which of you have had your brains enhanced?" I ask.

"Tezza, my PR person, has had her brain enhanced so she can make calculations quicker." She paused to think for a moment. "Only my personal consultant, HAL50, doesn't actually have bionics since he has an android body."

"But he has a human brain," HARV says. "So that has not been enhanced?"

Merinda shakes her head. "No, that would be an overkill. We on Mars are subtle."

"What about you?" I ask. "What are your enhancements, Merinda?"

"Certain areas of my brain have been tweaked to allow me to tap into my body's energies," Merinda tells us.

"Oh?"

Merinda touches me gently on the shoulder. My shoulder warms. "But this simply allows me to make people feel comfort. It's important that leaders be comforting."

"So it's possible that you or Tezza could detect Carol poking around in your brains?"

Merinda looks at me directly in the eyes. "Frankly, Zach, I have no idea."

"Tió, I can be a help to you there," Carol says in my head. "Besides, I've always wanted to go to Mars."

"It's worth the risk," HARV tells me.

"OK, Carol and I can be ready in two hours," I tell Merinda. "How long is the trip to Mars?"

"Roughly thirty Earth hours," Merinda says.

"Thirty hours and thirty-one minutes," HARV informs us.

"Like I said, roughly thirty hours," Merinda says. "Of course, we have 3-D printers onboard, so we can make you fresh clothing or personal items, if needed."

"My suit and underarmor have the latest in nanocleaning bots, so I am always fresh and clean," I tell her. "So I'm good. At least for two or three days."

I turn my attention to Carol. "But I take it you need a change of clothing?"

Carol nods. "Yeah, I am *not* wearing the same outfit for an entire trip."

Merinda smiles. "Carol, you will be happy to know we have a complete wardrobe bot on our ship. We can make you the finest of outfits."

Carol's face lights up. "I'm good to go then, I guess."

"OK, Carol, unfreeze Alicia." Turning my attention to HARV, I say, "Have you gotten any more information from the ship on Merinda's companions?"

HARV nods. "Yes, after Merinda prodded her ship some, SRIP did give me more data, but nothing beyond the basics: their favorite foods, their favorite colors, their favorite music…"

"SRIP likes to make sure we are all comfortable," Merinda says. "SRIP really does treat us well."

HARV's eyes start to blink quickly, a sign he's processing something. "Zach, the rest of Merinda's team is in the lobby. They look anxious. They will be here in three minutes."

Turning my attention to Carol, I say, "OK, unfreeze Alicia, and let's get this show on the road. I want to see if any of Merinda's people act more guarded around you."

"So do you want me to poke their brains?" Carol asks.

I shake my head. "Not yet. Just in case Tezza—with her bionic brain—is the potential killer, I don't want to tip her off." I smile. "Still, just seeing how they each react knowing you are a psi can be a help." Pointing at Alicia, I tell Carol, "Unfreeze her. We want everything normal when the rest get here."

"Wait!" Merinda says, finger raised. "How do you want Saturn and me to act?"

I shrug. "Business as usual. Saturn is safe, and all is good with the worlds."

Merinda takes a deep breath. "I can do that."

"Merinda's team is in the hallway," HARV informs us. "It is time, as they say, to get the show on the road."

I give Carol a nod.

"You can move, and everything is fine," she tells Alicia. "We are about to greet the rest of your crew. Everything is great."

Alicia snaps back to life. She gives a wide smile. "I am so happy our crew is back." Heading out of Merinda's room, she calls to us, "Come. Let's give them a proper greeting."

We all follow Alicia into the suite's living area. Maxxx, Tezza, and HAL50 are already in the room. Maxxx is a short, thick man with brown hair and a solid chin. He's the type of guy you can just tell is comfortable in a brawl. Tezza is a tall, slim woman with dark-brown hair and radiant blue eyes. A quick look and you know she's the type of woman who could sell snow to an Eskimo. HAL50 looks like a life-size Ken doll. He has just a hint of orange in his complexion to inform observers that he is an android. Of course, his plastic perfection should let even the daftest observer realize he's not human. Still, I guess his makers didn't want to take any chances.

The three of them smile when they see Merinda holding Saturn. Man, that woman is strong!

Tezza approaches Merinda and Saturn first. "Glad you are back safely," she says, petting a very content-looking Saturn.

"Yes, I am so happy I called Zachary and his team to help my team," Merinda says. She smiles widely as she addresses her people. "I am so pleased with Zach's performance, I have invited him and his aide, Carol, to go back to Mars with us for a reward."

Now, this was going to prove interesting, to see how the others would react to the news. History has taught me that security folks usually hate it when I am around. They don't appreciate me stomping on their territory.

Maxxx walks up to me, his face one giant grin. Patting me firmly on the back, he says, "It will be so great to have you on the trip! We can swap stories!"

Of course, history doesn't always repeat itself.

Looking over at Tezza, I see her eyes are wide open, her fist is clenched, and her hair is on edge. "So it's true you are canceling your appointment with the World Council over this man!" Tezza gasps and shouts at the same time.

There are a couple of ways I can handle this…

"Merinda, my leader, how could you cancel such an important meeting with the World Council?" Tezza asks, though from her tone, it is easy to tell this is more of a statement than a question.

If I were one of those macho PIs from the old days, I would have stepped in and offered some sort of reason, but as my old mentor used to say, a smart

PI knows when to step back and let others do the work. And smart PIs live longer. I decide to let Merinda handle this. I would just watch Tezza, and also Alicia, Maxxx, and HAL50. By watching, I may gain valuable clues about which one of them might want Merinda dead.

Merinda put her hand on Tezza's shoulder to comfort her. "TZ, my trusted advisor, Zach did such a brave and kind thing, I feel we need to reward him quickly. This way, we show the people of Earth how generous the people of Mars are—how we are good to our friends. I am sure the average Earth person relates much more to Zach than he or she does to a council member."

"True," I tell her. "I am just a regular working Joe." OK, yeah, that wasn't actually totally true. A lot of people don't really relate to what I do or how I relish things from the past, but still, I do have my fans.

Tezza's head and eyes shoot back and forth from Merinda to me, back to Merinda, back to me, and then settle on Merinda. She smiles. "Yes, yes—we can use this during our trip to Mars. I'll be able to get to know Zach better so I can present him in the best possible way. If we get the people of Earth on our side, we know the politicians will follow."

I figured it was in my best interest to let the comment pass. Looking at Carol, I think, "Any vibes from any of them?"

"No, but that might not mean anything because their brains are slightly different than the brains of people on Earth. I may have to adapt some to read them."

Turning my attention to Alicia, I ask, "How long until we are ready to roll?"

"Roll what?" she asks.

"He means, how long until we are ready for the trip to Mars?" HARV says, and then notes, "I am fluent in Zach-speak."

"Oh," Alicia says. "I've been in communication with our ship. He says it will be ready in ninety Earth minutes."

Since I have a little more time, I think maybe I can crack the case open, and therefore save a trip to Mars. I can poke a few egos and rattle a couple of mental cages to see what, if anything, shakes out. Yeah, not the subtlest PI work, for sure, but sometimes the hard play is the right play. Not only that, if it works, it would save me from having to explain to Electra that I was going to Mars.

I decide it would be best to shake Merinda's employee applecart a bit to see if anything falls out that I might be able to use against that employee. There is the direct, hard-poke approach and the subtler-poke approach. Since I didn't want to tip my hand too much, I go with the subtle touch.

"I'm glad I will be accompanying you all back to Mars," I say with a big waste-eating grin on my face. "I've never been to Mars. I hear it's amazing what you've done with the place." This is a classic PI trick of softening up a target before hitting it with a hard shot. I smile. "Of course, a lot of people would be uneasy traveling in an enclosed area for a couple of days with the world's last PI." I scan the faces in the room. I don't detect any noticeable ticks. "I hope none of you have anything to hide," I add.

Scanning again, I notice that Alicia is slightly hunched over and turning from my gaze. Hm, could the doting-personal-aide act be only an act? Heading over toward Alicia, I mention, "Alicia, you seem to have something on your mind."

"Zach, where are you going with this?" HARV asks in my mind.

"Yeah, tió." Carol mentally agrees. "I don't get any evil vibe from her at all."

I walk past HAL50 and Maxxx. I note that HAL50 readily moves to the side to let me pass. Maxxx hesitates for a moment, like he thinks he wants to say or do something, but he doesn't.

Reaching Alicia, who is now standing behind Merinda, I start my line of questioning. "What's going on, Alicia?"

Looking at her feet, she says, "Ah, nothing—business as usual. As you here on Earth used to say, everything is A-OK."

I smile. The history buff in me really appreciates the *A-OK*. Of course, she may have known I like history. She may have done that to intentionally get on my good side, to get me to let down my guard. Yeah, I do have a thing for the old days. They were simpler times when everybody wasn't wired to everything, but still you don't stay alive in this business for as long as I have if you get easily distracted.

"What are you hiding, Alicia?" I press.

"Nothing, nothing, nothing," she insists, still looking away from me.

"That's a lot of nothing," I tell her. "I kind of think that much nothing leads to something."

"I know you think that sounds cool, but don't push too hard," Carol warns.

I glance over quickly at Merinda, who is petting Saturn. I need to gauge her reaction. She seems content in letting this play out. Saturn has his ears perked up.

"You are hiding something, Alicia!" I insist.

Alicia turns and takes a step away from me. Yeah, she is definitely hiding something. She may not have been the one to threaten Merinda's life, but something isn't kosher with her. I have to find out what.

Lunging forward, I put my hand on her shoulder. "Talk to me," I order, as I try to spin her toward me with a tug.

Alicia resists my initial tug. That was a friendly warning tug. If she wants to play rougher, I am more than game. Grabbing her by the shoulder, I spin her firmly toward me. We are face-to-face. The kicker is, she has a knife with a shining fifteen-centimeter blade pressed against my throat.

"You want answers? I'll give you answers!" she screams.

I never would have pegged Alicia as the keep-a-knife-up-the-sleeve type. Now this was an interesting development.

"Alicia, what are you doing?" Merinda asks, her voice strong and unwavering.

Alicia presses the knife a bit closer to my throat. Her hand is shaking. Sweat beads on her brow. "I'm sorry, Merinda!" Alicia says, never taking her eyes off me.

I take a deep breath. I act relaxed and calm, hoping it will rub off on Alicia. "So, Alicia, what's on your mind?" I say slowly and calmly.

"Ah, ah—nothing," she stammers, knife still to my throat.

"Your mouth says nothing, but your knife says something else," I tell her.

"Smooth," HARV says cynically in my head.

"Agreed," Carol chimes in.

"Hey, you two. It's hard being extra witty with a knife to your jugular," I think back.

"You should be accustomed to situations like this," HARV says. "Jobs and Gates know you are attacked enough."

"Agreed," Carol chimes in again.

Yeah, I know it's probably not the best practice to be ignoring the angry lady with a knife to my throat. But something tells me that even though Alicia is worried and scared, she isn't a killer. It's a lot easier to draw a knife than to end a life.

"HARV, look at Alicia's salary and expenses, and see if anything doesn't add up."

"Curious, she makes a modest three thousand credits a pay cycle, yet she has well over a million credits in her accounts. She's not even hiding it all that well," HARV replies.

I need to play this right. Just because Alicia's not the type of lady who is used to stabbing people in the neck, that doesn't mean she wouldn't do it, especially if pushed too hard. I slide my left hand up slowly near Alicia's right arm. If she reacts violently to my next question, I need to be able to deflect her knife away from my body.

"So, Alicia, how does a low-paid personal aide get over a million credits saved up?" I ask.

"Oh, you probably should have left out the *low-paid*," Carol thinks to me.

"Agreed," HARV says in my mind.

Alicia drops her head and lets the knife fall. She turns to Merinda, sobbing. "I'm sorry! I'm sorry!" she cries, tossing herself at Merinda's feet.

"See, guys? That's why I am the professional PI and you guys work for me!" I think back to HARV and Carol.

"I don't get paid, so technically, I don't work for you," HARV says. "But I do find you entertaining."

"I work *with* you," Carol says.

Bringing my attention back to the lady that had a knife at my throat and the other lady whom I am here to protect, I tell Merinda bluntly, "My PI gut tells me Alicia has been e-embezzling cash from you."

Merinda looks down at Alicia sobbing at her feet. "Alicia, is this true?"

Alicia nods, eyes welling, tears streaming down her face. "Yes, the budget allocates a hundred thousand credits a month for flowers. Since I am so efficient, I am able to purchase lovely arrangements for a fraction of that cost."

"What are you planning with the extra cash?" I ask, walking up next to Alicia. (I thought about saying *dough* instead of *cash*, but figured that would confuse her.)

Alicia looks up at Merinda, her eyes swollen and pleading. "I've been saving for a dark market bionics implant. I want my arms to be bionic so I can be strong for you—to protect you as well as to serve you."

"I have confirmed that Alicia has had two appointments with a doctor Ferguson from Orbital City," HARV says. "He specializes in bionic implants in the arms, butt, and lips."

Merinda kneels down and rubs Alicia gently on the shoulder. "Oh, my dear Alicia. You don't need to do that for me."

Maxxx and Tezza head over toward us. I can't help but notice Maxxx is flexing his muscles some.

"Don't worry. I would never let any harm come to Merinda." Maxxx assures Alicia.

"Neither would I," Tezza says. "That would be terrible PR."

Merinda smiles at Alicia. "See, Alicia. I am perfectly safe. You don't need to augment yourself for me."

OK, was that it? Was that really all Alicia was guilty of—caring too much? Or could this all be an act?

I give Alicia the once over a couple of times. I'm still not 100 percent sure she is as innocent as she claims. Well, DOS—hardly anybody is as innocent as he or she claims. I just need to be as sure as I can be that she isn't the one Saturn heard thinking about harming Merinda.

"Carol, do you or Saturn pick up any bad vibes from Alicia?" I think.

"She's scared and ashamed," Carol thinks back to me. "But neither Saturn nor I feel she would be a danger to Merinda."

"Well, let's give her one more test. Concentrate on her. See if her thoughts give her away," I think.

Looking at Alicia, I bark, "Why does an innocent aide need to keep a knife up her sleeve?"

Alicia takes a defensive step backward. "I am an aide to Merinda, one of Mars's council members. We are on a potentially hostile planet. It is only natural I would be prepared to protect her."

"She seems sincere to Saturn and me," Carol thinks to me.

"Zach, I am not picking up any noticeable signs of lying," HARV says out loud. It was a good move on his part. Knowing we are watching her closely could coax another reaction out of Alicia. I like to believe HARV has picked up a thing or three from me.

Alicia takes another step back. With her hand over her heart, she says, "I would do anything to protect my Merinda." Looking me directly in the eyes, she says, "Yes, I would even kill for her if needed." Directing her glance at Merinda, "That is why I wanted to make myself stronger for you."

"I believe you," Merinda says, taking Alicia's hand.

"I believe her, too," HARV says.

"Me too," Carol says.

"Woof!" Saturn barks, which I take as a bark of confidence.

I'm still not quite ready to cross Alicia off the potential-killer list. After all, she was pretty darn quick to whip out that knife.

"You're good with a knife," I say, pointing at Alicia. "Not only did you draw it quickly, but you put it against my jugular like a person who knows how to wield a bladed weapon."

"Of course I do," Alicia says.

"We all do," Tezza says.

"It's a rite of passage on Mars," Maxxx adds.

"Huh?" I say, trying not to sound nearly as confused as I am.

"Earthlings know so little about us." HAL50 sighs.

Merinda glides over to me and takes my hand. "Zach, we on Mars have a huge cloned cattle industry. Martian steak is the finest on all the known planets."

That jars my memory. I once had a taste of Martian steak while I was working on a case for Ona Thompson, the richest woman on Earth. It's a steak that only the top 1 percent can afford.

"It is expensive," I say. "I will give you that." Actually, the steak does melt in your mouth and makes your taste buds dance and almost sing with joy, but I wasn't going to admit that.

"Our steak is so good because it is all hand raised and hand killed," Merinda insists. "Each citizen of Mars must do the training and volunteer on the ranches two days a cycle."

"Which we all proudly do," Alicia says.

Tezza, Maxxx, and HAL50 all nod in agreement.

Alicia touches her ear. "Good news, ma'am," she tells Merinda. "SRIP has contacted me. He is ready to take off early. He can leave now." Alicia looks at Merinda. "Is that OK, ma'am?" She turns her gaze to me. "Do you trust me now?"

Well, I never totally trust anybody except for Electra, Carol, and HARV, but in this case, I did believe Alicia. While a good PI never totally eliminates a suspect without unwavering evidence of his or her innocence, I certainly had to drop Alicia down on my potential-killer list.

"Yeah, I believe you," I tell Alicia.

Merinda puts a hand on my shoulder. "So, Zach, are you ready to head to Mars now?"

I could question Maxxx, Tezza, and HAL50 here on Earth, where I had the home-field advantage. Thing is, I'm guessing they might be more open and more apt to slip up if I casually questioned and observed them on the way to Mars.

"So we really can get to Mars in thirty hours and change?" I ask.

"Yes, thanks to Mars's advancement with the new ultra fusion propulsion systems, we can make the trip far faster than Earthlings ever dreamed," Tezza says, beaming.

HARV appears between Tezza and me. I can tell from the look on HARV's face he's about to go into what I can only describe as *annoying professor* mode. Normally, I am not a fan of being lectured to by HARV, but I figured this would be interesting, since I knew he was also going to lecture Tezza.

"The engines are actually not much larger than the engines that power hovers and land-based vehicles, yet they are much more powerful. For the first half of the trip, we will accelerate to speeds that were only a sci-fi writer's pipe dream as little as forty years ago. Once we reach the halfway point, the ship will slowly decelerate on its approach to Mars. Despite generating this massive amount of energy, the engines are shielded by force fields preventing them from killing their passengers. I could give more details, but I know those would be lost on most of you. I'm sure Zach is already confused," HARV says in a dry, monotone voice.

"True," I say with a nod. "While I do enjoy driving my car, I don't have much of an idea about how it works. I just push the on button and go."

"Yes." HARV sighs. "In that respect, Zach is a typical human. He is so reliant on science but doesn't really understand it all that well," HARV pauses for a moment, "at least with the true sciences, those that use a lot of math. Zach is actually fairly knowledgeable in biology, because he knows where to hit people to do the most damage. But biology is a softer science."

"I'm also pretty good at psychology," I note.

HARV snickers. "Please, that barely classifies as a science."

Tezza steps forward to go face-to-face with HARV. "Yes, that's why we on Mars are different. We are beings that have been touched by science. After all, we all have bionics, but we are also in tune with our natural artistic sides. Hence the reason we create such lovely goods and such amazing pieces of technology, like our ship."

"I'll give you credit for the esoteric crafts," HARV says. "With those types of goods, beauty and use is in the eye of the beholder. As for your ship, if it weren't for the Gladians, you and the people of Earth would be much more restricted in your space travel. It's really more of an accomplishment for interplanetary cooperation than Mars or Earth technology," HARV says.

Tezza crosses her arms in defiance. "While the Gladians may have shared their engine designs with us, the SRIP interface is all ours."

HARV pauses for a moment. I know he is formulating his reply. "While a computer interface is of course needed, I've been talking with the SRIP interface. It doesn't seem all that special to me. In fact, I think it is a bit slow and one-dimensional. It really isn't much different than the standard Bob interface most Earthlings, as you call them, use to update their calendars and perform other trivial feats."

Merinda, being the leader, sees where this is heading and steps forward. "While this debate is both educational and spirited, I have called for the hotel's hover to take us to the New Frisco spaceport. It will pick us up on the roof. I suggest we start to head there now."

I know we have to get moving, but still there's no reason why HARV can't poke Tezza a bit while we are moving. It could help expose any weaknesses. Of course, it could also irk her off and cause her to clam up.

OK, I'm enjoying HARV's mental grilling of Tezza. After all, it was giving me insight into how Tezza thinks—insight about whether she might be capable of hurting Merinda. But I also know it is time to start heading to Mars. When the suspects were in their more familiar environment, there was a better chance of them slipping up.

"Merinda is right," I say. "Let's get to the roof. I'm anxious to see this spaceship of yours. HARV, please go into observation mode until further notice."

HARV glares at me. His forehead furrows to show his disdain. "As you wish," he says as he disappears.

"Zach, you still want me to continue poking Tezza to see what I might stir up?" HARV asks in my mind.

"Sure, let's just move and poke," I think back. "Let's wait until we get on the elevator until you go at her again."

Merinda and her team are very organized. It is not long until we are on the elevator heading up to the roof. Looking over Merinda and her crew, I have to admit they all look relaxed and seem generally happy about heading back to Mars. Of course, I wasn't going to let that happiness last, at least not for Tezza, at least not right now.

"OK, HARV. You can start your mental softening up of Tezza," I think to him as we start gliding upward.

No answer.

"Zach to HARV…Come on HARV, this is what you do best, drive humans and near humans crazy."

Still no answer, which was unusual to say the least. HARV almost always answers, even the times I don't want him to answer.

"HARV?"

Merinda must have noticed a look of concern on my face. She hands Saturn to Alicia and walks over to me.

"Zach, are you OK?" She asks, touching me gently on the shoulder.

I hesitate for a nano, and then say, "I kind of expect HARV to be back."

Tezza rolls her eyes. "I am so glad that annoying simulated human isn't here. I don't know how any of you can deal with him."

"He is an acquired taste," I say slowly, itching my head.

"I find him entertaining," Maxxx says.

"I'm with Tezza. I don't like him," HAL50 chimes in. "He gives machines a bad name."

"HARV? Where are you?" I think.

"Tió, I can't sense him, either," Carol thinks.

The numbers 00000000000000000000 flash across my eyes. The numbers change to 0101010101. Then they become 11111111111111111.

I see the message scroll across my eyes: Z A C H I A M U N D E R S O M E S O R T O F D E N I A L O F S E R V I C E A T T A C K.

This is something that doesn't happen very often. It takes a pretty sophisticated attack to slow down HARV a fraction of a nanosecond. Though I like to think I can solve most crimes without HARV, I have to admit he is handy to have around. The question is now, what's the best way for me to get him back?

10

We get out of the elevator and onto the hotel's rooftop. I can see the shuttle-craft coming to take us to Merinda's ship. All in all, I would say I am making progress on the case—except, of course, now HARV is under some sort of attack.

"HARV, are you still with us?" I think.

Nothing.

"Come on, HARV!" I mentally coax.

I hear in my mind three quick beeps, three long beeps, and then three quick beeps. It's an SOS. For HARV to resort to Morse code, this has to be even worse than I thought.

Merinda gazes over at me. "Zach, are you OK?"

"Yeah, buddy. You look kind of pale," Maxxx notes.

"I'm fine," I halfheartedly reassure them. Rubbing my stomach, I tell them, "I just grabbed a bad taco at the taco hover."

Merinda moves over to me and places her hand over my stomach. "Perhaps I can help," she says calmly.

"Ah, OK, but usually there's just one thing that relieves this," I tell her.

"Zach, just relax," I hear Merinda say in my head. "The bionics in my brain give me psi powers. One of my abilities is to heal. I can sense what's going on between you and HARV. You need to let me heal you both."

"Ah, how?" I ask. "You going to reboot my brain?"

Merinda smiles. "Actually, yes," she thinks.

"That could work!" Carol says in my head. DOS, my mind is getting congested.

I know in the old days, back when a computer was having problems, a reboot would often do the trick. Still, I couldn't say I was thrilled about having my mind rebooted.

"Don't be a baby," Carol thinks to me. "You've had me and so many other psis playing around with your white and gray matter, this is no big deal. If you want, I can reboot you."

"Carol, I know you have a powerful mind, but my mind is built for healing," Merinda thinks.

"The shuttle will be on the ground in one minute," Alicia informs us.

"Zach, I can have you feeling better by then," Merinda tells me. Holding out her hand, she says, "Trust me."

I take a deep breath, and then another. "HARV?" I think out one last time.

Once again all I hear is three quick beeps, three slow beeps, and three quick beeps.

"Help me," I tell Merinda.

Merinda puts a hand on my midsection and another on my forehead. "Just relax, Zach."

I feel warmth on my head and in my gut. Not just the warmth from Merinda's touch, but an extra type of warmth that I can only describe as hot cocoa on a cold day. My entire body starts to relax.

The next thing I know, Carol is standing behind me for support. I'm not sure why, until my knees buckle.

I feel a slight jostle from behind. "Come on, tió, wake up. You're heavy."

"Carol, give him a second to recover," I hear Merinda order.

The first thing I see when I open my eyes are Merinda's incredibly green eyes. She smiles. "Welcome back. How do you feel?"

"HARV, are you in there?"

The numbers 1…2…3 scroll in front of my eyes. "I'm back, Zach."

"I'm fine. Thank you, Merinda."

"Why did you have to make him pass out to fix an upset stomach?" HAL50 asks.

"I wanted to give him a complete reset," Merinda says. "It's good for the body and the soul."

"Now that Mr. Johnson's tummy ache is over, may I suggest we head to our ship?" Tezza says, pointing at the shuttle that has just landed.

"Of course," Merinda says.

We were going to have to figure out who or what attacked HARV. That would lead us closer to Merinda's would-be attacker. But something else was troubling me: Merinda was much more powerful than I had thought. I wasn't sure I liked the fact that I was just finding out now that she could read minds and project her thoughts. The question is what, if anything, am I going to do about it?

The trip from the shuttle to Merinda's rocket goes surprisingly smoothly. Nobody attacks or tries to kill me or anybody else. That is good because it gives me time to think. I'm a little worried that Merinda never told me she could read and, to some extent, control minds. I decide to keep quiet about it until we board her ship.

The ship itself, while being mega cool, since after all, it is a rocket ship to Mars, doesn't actually look like anything *that* special from the outside: just a long streamlined metal bullet. I am sure HARV would tell me it's not really made out of metal, but whatever it was made of was shining and silver. Like I said, ultra cool, but nothing special in this day and age of teleporting.

The inside of the ship reminds me of those luxury hover buses that rock and video stars use when touring the country. I was on one of those once when I worked a case for the clones of the Still Grateful Dead. This was a little bigger and roomier (and not nearly as smoky), but still pretty much the same.

"Welcome to our ship, SRIP," Merinda tells me with a smile, as we enter the common area.

"I have made all the necessary calculations and arrangements for our return to Mars," a semirobotic voice informs us over the ship's intercom. "Just tell me when you wish to take off."

"Thank you, SRIP," Merinda says. Merinda turns to me. "Private quarters are in the back of SRIP. I will have Alicia show you and Carol to your rooms. Zachary, when we take off, you may either be in your room in the back of the ship or in the common seating area near the front. Wherever you think you would be the most comfortable."

"You know what would make me really comfortable?" I ask, locking eyes with Merinda.

She looks down without looking away. "You are wondering why I did not tell you more about my abilities," she says.

"Yeah," I tell her. "A PI's best weapon is information. Without having complete information, it's like fighting a ninja with one hand tied behind your back."

"You are such a drama king," HARV says.

Before Merinda can respond, Alicia steps between us. Alicia's eyes are wide open, and her hair is standing on end. "Ms. Merinda is a member of the Mars High Council. For all intents and purposes, she is royalty. She does not have to tell you anything more than she thinks you need to know. If she does not think you need to know it, then you do not need to know." Alicia grabs me by the shoulder. "Got it?"

On one hand, I am impressed by Alicia's loyalty to her boss. On the other hand, I hate having people grab me. It's just so rude.

Looking over Alicia to Merinda, I ask, "Are you going to answer my question and handle this?" I move my head toward Alicia so Merinda understands what—well, who—I mean by *this*.

"Zach, I'm sorry," Merinda says.

"For not giving me information or for your aide threatening me?"

"Technically, she hasn't threatened you," Maxxx says.

"She's just doing what we're all thinking," Tezza says. "You are a bit overbearing."

"I'm actually loving this," HAL50 smirks.

Once again I find myself toe-to-toe and chin-to-eyes with an angry Alicia..

"Want me to mentally blast her?" Carol asks again in my head.

"No, I need to handle this myself, Carol. Pay attention to the others, though, and see how they react."

Not wanting to let this go on any longer, I decide to put a hard stop on the situation. I grab the wrist of Alicia's hand—the one holding me. In one fluid motion, I spin backward and into Alicia, locking her underarm on top of my shoulder. I bend and pull her forward, flipping her over my shoulder. Alicia hits the floor with a very satisfying thud.

"That will teach you once and for all not to mess with me!" I tell her firmly.

Glancing up quickly at Alicia's coworkers, I notice Maxxx has a wry smile on his face. Tezza is shaking her head, but she doesn't look very upset with me. HAL50 is the interesting one. He is just standing there, but I notice his orangish robotic fists are clenching.

"Carol, can you pick up anything from HAL50?" I think.

"His brain is human, but being in that android shell makes it harder," Carol thinks back.

"Try!" I think. "Team up with HARV."

"Zach, that is actually a decent idea," HARV thinks.

You don't live as long as I have doing the job I do without one or two decent ideas. But I realize I don't need HARV and Carol to team up to deduce what HAL50 is about to do. His eyes narrow and focus on me. I have seen that look often. He is getting ready to charge. The only thing that would make it more obvious would be if his back foot started to twitch.

"Never mind," I tell HARV and Carol with my mind. "He's going to rush me."

"Yes, we have come to the same conclusion," I hear them echo in my mind, an eerie HARV-and-Carol mix.

Before I have time to contemplate how mega creepy that is, HAL50 races at me, hands now curled into fists. "Leave her alone, you cad!" he shouts.

I'm a fairly big guy: nearly two meters tall and around ninety kilograms. HAL50, though, is bigger than I am. Plus, I've tangled with enough pure androids in my life to know they are stronger than normal humans. Luckily, I have two things going for me. First, I played a bit of quarterback in high school, back in the day before they declared football too dangerous and replaced human players with androids. (Of course, an underground human football league still thrives.) Not to mention, I do get attacked a lot. The bottom line is I am used to being rushed by bigger guys. Second, as anybody can tell you, I'm not normal—not even close.

"HARV, are you powering up my muscles if I need an extra boost?" I think, keeping one eye on the charging android.

"Of course, Zach."

Even with HARV's boost, I need to time this right. Just as HAL50 reaches me, I drop my shoulder down to a level below his waist. As HAL50 hits my shoulder, I grab his back with both my hands and arch my back. My move sends him flying over me, crashing on the ground maybe half a meter past where Alicia is lying.

"Sweet move," I hear Maxxx say.

"OK, we're not giving Mars a good name here," Tezza says.

"People, Zachary is our guest. Remember, he saved Saturn," Merinda says sternly. "Don't make me give you all a mental time-out!"

"Woof!" Saturn agrees.

HAL50 doesn't seem to hear anything anyone says. He is furious. From the ground, his android arms telescope out and grab me by my ankles.

"I did not know he could do that," Tezza says.

Just lovely, I think. I need to end this fast. Of course, the question of the moment is how?

I can feel HAL50 tightening his viselike grip around my ankles. My underarmor is protecting me for now, but I can't let this go on much longer. Yeah, I could pop my gun into my hand and shoot him, but that would be too drastic of a move, especially since I know that HAL50 is doing this to defend Alicia. I have to give him kudos for that. Of course there's a difference between giving a guy—well, an android with a guy's brain—kudos, and letting it break your ankles.

"Zach, do you wish for me to help?" Merinda thinks to me.

"You can't go wrong with Merinda's help," Saturn thinks.

"I can help, too!" Carol thinks.

"I am sure I can do something, also," HARV transmits to my brain. "After all, I do rule when it comes to dealing with machines."

"OK, there are way too many people in my head!" I mentally scream. "This is more annoying than being squeezed by an android with a human brain!"

"Everybody, time-out!" Merinda shouts.

The next thing I know, Merinda is tapping me on the shoulder. "Zach! Zach! Mars to Zach. Time to wake up!"

I open my eyes to see Merinda standing in front of me, smiling. Saturn is asleep, curled up in a ball near her feet. Looking around, I notice HAL50 has released his grip on me. He is now asleep on the floor. In fact, everybody else in the room, including HARV, is asleep on his or her feet.

"I thought everybody could use a little time-out," Merinda says.

"I'm not going to argue with you on that one," I tell her. Though I have to say I am a little off put by how easily she can stop people in their tracks. Pointing to HARV and Carol, I note, "Those two aren't easy to control."

Merinda nods. "Yes, I believe the bionics in my mind, combined with my Martian DNA, make certain parts of my mind quite powerful. I am hard to resist. Even SRIP is asleep."

"So then why not probe the minds of your people to see who is trying to harm you?"

Merinda sighs. "I do try to stay out of the minds of those around me."

"Yeah, but once Saturn heard that somebody wanted to harm you, I would think you'd at least try to pick their brains. DOS, you can probably make them talk."

Merinda looks away from me. "I have to admit, Zach, I did try. But none of them seem to know anything. Whoever the guilty person is, he or she may somehow be immune to that part of my power."

Looking around at the sleeping Carol, HARV, Maxxx, Tezza, and HAL50, I find that hard to believe. Then, gazing out of one of the windows of the ship, I notice the people around the ship are also asleep on their feet.

"Wait, you put everybody in the area to sleep?" I say.

"Well, not quite," Merinda answers.

I point out the window. "Look out there. All the ground crew is asleep."

Merinda nods. "Yeah, well…Zach, I haven't quite told you the entire story. Right now your entire planet is asleep."

look around Merinda's ship to see that everybody, except Merinda and I, are asleep on his or her feet. Peering out the window, I see the same thing. Just for kicks, I activate my wrist communicator to scan for any broadcast. Total silence.

"Impressive," I tell Merinda.

Merinda gives me a wry smile. "I do have to admit it comes in handy at times."

"It would have been nice, though, if you had told me about these extra powers of yours," I say bluntly.

Merinda locks her big, green eyes on me. "Frankly, Zach, I didn't want to cloud the issue."

"Cloud the issue? Your powers are a big part of the issue!" Waving at everybody sleeping, I add, "Power like this makes you a threat."

Merinda tightens her glare on me. "Don't you think I know that!" she blares. She takes a deep breath and calms a bit. "Zach, it isn't your place to ponder why somebody might want to harm me. It's your job to figure out who it is, despite his or her reason."

Standing my mental ground, I retort, "Merinda, knowing *why* they might want to kill you helps me determine *who* might want to kill you."

Merinda turns away from me. "Yes, I see that now. I should have given you full disclosure on the true nature of my power."

"Here's the thing, Merinda. Haven't you used your powers to probe your people?"

Merinda nods. "I told you they all deny any involvement. Somehow, whoever this is, is immune to my power."

Looking around the room at the sleeping people, I find that hard to believe. "OK, how long do we have until they wake up?"

"They will sleep for as long as I will them to, but I find anything more than a few minutes will cause a dissonance. So I try not to keep subjects sleeping for more than ten minutes. It's easy to justify in their minds why they missed ten minutes of their day."

"Ah, OK, if you say so."

I didn't have a lot of time, but I still wanted to take some advantage of the situation. "Please, take me to HAL50's quarters."

"It's this way," Merinda says, moving toward a door at the end of the common area we are in. "Why his room?"

"One, he was the last member of your team to attack me. Two, he has a human brain in an android body. If you ask me, that's asking for trouble with a capital T."

We reach the door to HAL50's quarters. Merinda waves her hand over the lock and the door pops open. Walking into the room, the first thing I notice is that there is no bed.

"Where's the bed?" I ask.

"HAL50 only needs an hour of sleep each day, which he takes sitting down."

Looking around the room, it's not just missing a bed. The place is pretty barren. It has an old wooden chair and desk, and nothing else. There are two doors in the back of the room. I assume the small one leads to a closet. The other door must lead to a bathroom.

"Each of the walls is an information screen?" I ask, heading toward the door I believe is a closet.

"Yes, of course," Merinda says.

I slide open the closet door to reveal a row of brown suits. Rubbing my hands over the suits' material (and checking the pockets), they are all smooth and expensive feeling. "These are real silk."

"HAL50 likes to look his best," Merinda says. "Those suits are handmade on Mars."

Pointing to the other door, I say, "That's a bathroom, right?"

Merinda nods as she follows me toward the door.

Walking into the bathroom, I can't help but ask, "Why does an android need a bathroom?"

"Well, this room was designed for nonandroids. Plus, HAL50 likes to keep it for company."

I move to an old-fashioned mirror and medicine cabinet on the wall over the sink. Sliding the door open, I notice the shelves are bare except for an old-fashioned barber's razor with a jet-black handle. I only realize what the razor is from my sense of fascination with things from the old days. I take the razor and flick it open to expose the shiny metal blade. Taking a strand of hair from my head, I run it over the blade. The hair splits in two. Now what does an android need with a really sharp razor?

Looking at the old barber's razor glistening in my hand, I can't help thinking, what the DOS does an android need with a razor? Showing the razor to Merinda, I say, "OK, I can understand why an android would want a bathroom for guests, but why in Asimov's name would an android need a razor?"

Merinda shrugs. "Androids have weird tastes."

OK, the razor wasn't exactly a smoking hand laser, but it was something. Now I needed to see if I could find more *something* on the other potential killers. "Do we have time to check Tezza's room?" I ask.

Merinda nods as she leads me back into the main area of the ship, past all the sleeping people. "Of course."

We enter Tezza's room as I try not to think too hard about the repercussions of having a client who can put everybody to sleep on a whim. Tezza's room is the opposite of HAL50's. It is crammed with a huge king-size bed covered with pillows and a menagerie of stuffed-animal cats, a row of dressers, and lots of old mirrors. And everything is red. Her wall monitors are all on, with positive messages scrolling across them: "You are the best! Today is the first day of the rest of your life—conquer! The secret to success is to not give up! Success is 0.1 percent inspiration and 99.9 percent sweat. Ladies don't sweat. They perspire."

Pointing to a closet in the corner, Merinda tells me, "Tezza's room is the one with the wardrobe bot. Tezza is a wizard with it."

Right now though I am more interested in the stuffed animals on the bed. "Never pictured Tezza as a stuffed-animal kind of gal," I say, walking toward the bed. I'm not sure why the zoo of stuffed cats on her bed fascinates me so much.

"Each of these stuffed cats was handmade on Mars," Merinda says proudly.

Something about this stuffed Siamese doesn't feel right. It seems to have more weight than I would think a stuffed thingamajig should have.

"It feels heavy," I say.

"That's the great Mars handmade quality," Merinda assures me.

Rubbing my hand down the stuffed toy, I feel something decidedly solid in the tummy area. I use both hands to knead the object close to the surface of the stuffed animal. The very distinct form of a knife protrudes from the cloth lining. I show the form to Merinda.

"Looks like Tezza has issues," I tell her bluntly.

Merinda crosses her arms and sighs. "You have no idea why she keeps a knife in a stuffed animal. It could be a perfectly innocent reason."

On a whim, I drop the Siamese on the bed and pick up another stuffed cat—this one's a fat, yellow tabby with big cartoony eyes. Once again, being a trivia buff of the old days, I recognize this as Garfield. Feeling around Garfield's stuffing, I clearly feel another rough object. Moving that object with my hand, I determine it's another knife.

"This one has a knife in it too," I tell Merinda.

"OK, I admit that is odd, especially since Mars hasn't purchased licensing rights to Garfield."

"Yeah, *that's* what makes this odd," I say, not trying one bit to mask the sarcasm in my voice.

Showing the stuffed Garfield with the knife to Merinda, I say, "You do realize this isn't at all normal, right? Or is this how you stuff your stuffed animals on Mars?"

Merinda shakes her head. "I told you, Zach, that animal wasn't made on Mars. We don't have the licensing rights. We on Mars are very strict about licensing rights. Very few of our people are lawyers. That is why we are such a happy planet."

Sure enough, I look at a tag on the cat's foot, and it clearly reads, "Made on the Moon."

"How long have you had everybody asleep for?" I ask.

Merinda shrugs. "No idea. I have to admit this is the longest I've had everybody sleeping. Why do you ask?"

"If we have time, I figure I might as well check out Maxxx's room."

"You don't need to search Tezza's room more?" Merinda asks me.

I shake my head. "Nah, I don't think I can find anything stranger than stuffed animals with knives in them. I figure I'll check out Maxxx to see if he has any knives in his room. Since I'm sensing a theme here."

Merinda walks over to a wall. "Maxxx's room is connected to Tezza's." She touches the wall and a door appears.

"Isn't that kind of odd?" I say.

Merinda shrugs. "They are technically brother and sister. So they like to be close to each other."

Walking toward the door, I say, "Ah, aren't you all clones on Mars?"

Merinda places her palm on the door. It pops open. "Yes, we are clones. But there are many genetic lines. I'm from the 1616 line. They are from the 0808 line. Those of us from the same line tend to be closer. It gives us a sense of family."

"If you say so," I tell her, walking into the room connected to Tezza's.

This room is filled with weights. Not today's modern antigrav weights, but good old-fashioned metal weights. There are a few assorted punching bags, a treadmill, and an old stationary bike.

"Ah, I thought this was Maxxx's room, not the gym," I say, walking toward a wall that has a row of pegs traversing it.

"This is Maxxx's room. He likes to be in tip-top shape. He believes the old ways of training are the best."

"Where does he sleep?" I ask, drawing closer to the wall with pegs. I figure it's a climbing wall.

"He has a yoga mat he rolls on the floor. He says it's great for his back."

Upon reaching the wall, a closer inspection reveals that each of the pegs is actually a knife handle imbedded into the wall.

Yep, it was now official. All of Merinda's people have a thing for knives.

"So do you have knives in your room also?" I ask Merinda without looking at her.

I don't get a response. Turning my attention away from the knives lining the wall, I see Merinda squinting and holding her head.

"What's wrong?" I ask her.

Merinda shakes her head, her eyes still not fully open. "I have this buzzing in my brain. I may be pushing my powers too much."

I walk over to her and put a hand on her shoulder. "Maybe you should just wake everybody up now?"

"That won't be necessary," I hear the very familiar voice of Maxxx say behind me.

Turning, I see Maxxx, Tezza, Alicia, HAL50, and Carol walking into the room. To complete the party, HARV appears.

"What the DOS has been going on?" HARV asks.

"Yeah, why are you in my room?" Maxxx asks.

"Why did you come from my room?" Tezza asks.

Glancing back at Merinda, I think to her, "Hey, I thought everybody slept until you woke them?"

Merinda doesn't answer me. She just leans her head forward, pinching the ridge of her nose between two fingers.

"Tió, what are you thinking to Merinda?" Carol asks in my mind.

Maxxx, Tezza, and HAL50 storm up to me while Alicia heads toward Merinda.

"Merinda, are you OK?" Alicia asks.

Maxxx curls a hand into a fist. "I repeat, what are you doing in my room?"

"Yeah, and what happened to us?" HAL50 adds. "I repeat! What happened to us?" HAL50 demands.

The others all fixate their glares on us. Tezza, Maxxx, and HAL50 are red and ridged with anger. Alicia looks frantic and confused. My team of Carol and HARV are somewhere in between.

Saturn just stands there, staring up at us.

Merinda and I exchange glances. I don't need words or telepathy to know she is blindsided by this turn of events. She was still expecting everybody to be asleep as she commanded. Taking a quick glance out the window in Maxxx's room, I notice that everybody outside is still motionless.

"Why are you in my room?" Maxxx asks firmly. "Merinda, I know you are my leader, but we on Mars value our freedom and independence. I consider this an invasion of privacy!"

"Because it *is* an invasion of privacy!" Tezza adds, her face growing redder by the moment.

I decide here that the best defense is to go on the offense. "Here's the deal," I say firmly. "There has been a threat to Merinda's life. It was a threat made by one of you!" I accent that last statement by pointing dramatically at Merinda's crew.

"Threat by who?" Alicia asks.

"By whom," HARV corrects, being helpful as always.

I soften my stance a bit. "That's the kicker. I'm not sure who the *who* is," I tell the crowd.

They all murmur.

"Then how do you know there was a threat?" HAL50 asks.

"Yeah," Maxxx adds.

I point to Saturn. "Saturn picked up threatening thoughts."

"Wait, so you are investigating us on a thought the dog *thought* he heard?" Tezza says, not even trying to cover up the disdain in her voice.

"OK, when you say it like that, it does sound a tad whacky," I admit.

"I know what I heard in my mind!" Saturn thinks to all of us.

"And you all have to admit that Saturn is quite perceptive," Merinda says.

"Yeah, for a freaking dog!" HAL50 says. "But I've still caught him drinking out of the toilet!"

"Hey! It was just that one time, and I was thirsty, and it was clean!" Saturn protests. "This world is still biased against beings that don't have hands and opposable thumbs!"

I think about how I could play this. I could be coy. I could still be on the offensive. Like my old mentor used to say, when in doubt, be offensive.

"I found enough knives in all of your rooms to make you all suspects!" I say with conviction.

"Wait, you went through all of our rooms?" Tezza exclaims.

"Well, not Alicia's. I didn't need to. Not that I'm certain she's innocent, but I've seen her love of knives up close and personal. But yeah, I had Merinda give you all naps so I could work in peace. That's when I found you all have enough knives to start a Ginsu store."

"Of course we all have some kind of knife! We're from the Mars working class!" Tezza says. "Remember, Knives are part of what makes us *us*."

"She is right," Merinda says to me. "My people pride themselves on always having their knives handy."

…."Okay, so the knives are the best clues…." I admit.

"Zach in a world were we hardly ever have to flush our own tiolets or open our own doors we use knives as a reminder that it's good to do some things by hand."

"You could just open your own doors," I suggest.

That statement somehow sends my mind off in another direction. "HARV, how do the doors in this ship work?"

"Well, SRIP wasn't very forthcoming with any information, but a brief scan shows they are computer controlled."

"What if the computer is down?" I ask.

"Scanning, I see there are manual override buttons on the wall next to the doors." HARV answers.

Suddenly, it hit me. I knew where those threatening thoughts were coming from.

12

Putting all the pieces together, something hit me. If Merinda's intelligent ship, SRIP, had been sleeping like the rest of the world, it wouldn't have been able to open the doors to Merinda's crewmembers' rooms. That meant, at the very least, SRIP had been deceiving us.

"HARV, can this SRIP communicate with the crew telepathically?" I think to HARV.

"I assume so," HARV thinks back to me.

"Of course it can," Merinda thinks back to both of us. "SRIP was designed by Mars's technology, with the help of the Gladians and the psis on the moon, to read our thoughts in order to anticipate our needs."

"Wait, I thought the moon and Mars didn't get along," I think.

"When it comes to matters of the mind, we do cooperate," Merinda thinks.

"Yes, psis do share a common bond," Carol chimes in mentally.

OK, my very educated guess is that for some reason, Merinda's ship wants her dead. The thing is, I didn't have a motive, or for that matter, proof. I am going to have to play this coyly. I need to find out why a spaceship, even an intelligent one, would want to kill anybody. This is going to be trickier than dealing with humans and humanoids. At least with them, you could see them—read their faces and judge their actions. Plus, when push comes to push harder, why would an intelligent ship want to kill anybody?

"OK, Johnson, what's the story?" HAL50 says, poking me with a finger. "What gives you the right to be snooping around our rooms?"

I take a step back. I don't appreciate being poked. But before I can do anything, HARV appears between us.

"Ah, Mr. HAL50, I feel obligated to inform you that room belongs to the people of Mars, not you. If your leader, Merinda, feels threatened, then of course Zach has every right to examine all your rooms because they are actually her rooms she lets you use. I can show you the Mars charter, if you wish," HARV says, in typical longwinded HARV form.

"So, Zach, do you know who the potential killer is?" Alicia asks.

I shake my head. "Not yet, but I am going to question you each individually now. I think between Carol, HARV, and I, we should be able to crack whichever one of you it is."

"It's surely not me," Alicia says. "I've been nothing but loyal."

"It's not me, either," Tezza says. "It would be a PR nightmare."

"Obviously it's not me," Maxxx says. "After all, I *am* her security."

The three of them look at HAL50.

"Oh sure, blame the android with the human brain. It's always our fault," HAL50 moans.

"Nobody is blaming anybody, yet!" I say sharply. "Not until after I question you all."

I think to HARV, "HARV, as Carol and I question them, I need you to get as close as you can to SRIP to see if you can figure out what type of motive it might have."

"Or what type of means it might have," HARV adds.

"If I may interrupt you humans and near humans," SRIP calls over the intercom system. "I calculate this is an optimal time to take off. Now that Madam Merinda has woken up the good people of Earth, I suggest we launch ASAP."

Merinda turns to me. "Zach, are you ready to head to Mars?"

Now this is a bit dicey. I certainly don't want to let on that I am on to SRIP being sneaky at best, murderous at worse. The catch is, if SRIP really intends to kill Merinda, letting him blast us off into space where we would be at SRIP's mercy probably isn't the hottest idea. Of course, if I am going to maintain the facade of questioning Merinda's human and near-human crew, having SRIP take off might cause him to let his guard down.

Merinda keeps her focus on me. "Zach, are you ready to head to Mars?" she repeats.

There's no way I am eager to be blasted into space by an intelligent ship I suspect wants Merinda dead. Of course, I don't want to tip my hand.

"HARV, is everybody awake now?"

"Yes, Zach, everybody is awake. They have been for a while."

"Carol, I need you to mentally reach out to ground control and have them ground this flight."

"Madam Merinda!" SRIP says. "I suggest we take off while the conditions are so perfect."

"Well, Zach?" Merinda asks me.

"Ah, well," I say as slowly as I can.

"Well put," Tezza says.

"Man, I hope we're not paying this guy a lot," HAL50 groans.

"I like Zach!" Maxxx adds.

"Give me a nano," Carol thinks back to me. She stands steady, in deep concentration. A sly smile creeps across her lips. "Done!"

Before I can say anything, SRIP informs us all, "This is most unfortunate. According to Earth ground control, all flights are suspended until further notice. Apparently, there is excess sunspot activity that could hamper some electronics."

"Looks like we are Earthbound for a bit," I say.

"Actually, our technology is far ahead of Earth's when it comes to space travel," SRIP says confidently. "I am sure I can blast off and navigate without any problems."

"That's true," Tezza agrees. "We on Mars use space travel more than Earth does, so we are quite advanced."

I shake my head. "No, I don't think it's such a good idea to blast off when Earth ground control says no. We certainly don't want to start an interplanetary incident."

Alicia takes a step forward. "Oh, I see what's going on here." She thrusts a finger at Carol. "He used the mind-bending witch here to force ground control to keep us here."

I shrug. "True," I admit. "I am not overly anxious to be blasted into space, trapped in an enclosed area with a possible killer."

"It figures he'd use the mind witch," Tezza barks. "Psis and Martians just don't get along."

"Hence our trouble with the moon," Maxxx says.

"The relationship between Mars and the moon has nothing to do with this," I say in my calmest voice. "Carol is a tool in my arsenal that I use—"

"What?" Carol says, glaring at me, leaning toward me with her face turning red. "I'm just a tool?"

I hold up a hand to her. "Poor choice of words," I acknowledge with a nod.

Carol relaxes her stance. Her face returns to its normal light-golden-brown color. Saturn jumps into her arms and gives her a reassuring lick. Yeah, I like that dog.

"So you admit to manipulating the situation!" HAL50 says.

The good news is, I can be pretty certain SRIP doesn't suspect that I suspect him. The bad news is, I had just pretty much managed to get all of Merinda's staff and crew angry with me.

"HARV, any luck finding anything about SRIP's programming?" I think.

"Sorry, Zach. So far, I have less than zilch. I can't get any read on this computer. I find it very upsetting."

Just then it hit me. Maybe I had been going about this the wrong way. Maybe it was time to drop the facade and poke the e-tiger.

"Madam Merinda, do you wish me to ignore Earth authorities and take off to Mars?" SRIP coaxes. "I do not need their guidance or, for that matter, their permissions."

"Well, Zach, what do you think?" Merinda asks me.

"Probably not a good idea to irk ground control," I say in my most serious voice. "We're in no hurry. Certainly no need to create an incident. Especially since you will need to bring me back to Earth."

"Zach raises a fine point," Merinda says.

"And of course, my lady, Merinda, makes the wisest choice," Alicia agrees.

"No need in making my PR job even harder," Tezza agrees.

"I'm in no hurry," Maxxx says.

HAL50 just shrugs.

"Woof!" Saturn barks in agreement.

The good news is, that for once I had all of Merinda's people kind of on my side, at least as much on my side as a group of people who think I suspect one of them to be a murderer can be on my side. The challenging news is, I'm starting to think the only way I can get to SRIP is out-and-out accusing him of being the possible killer.

"HARV, you got anything out of SRIP? Any way to pick its brain?" I mentally ask.

The word *nada* rolls across my eyes.

I take a deep breath.

"Tió, what are you thinking?" Carol asks in my mind. She concentrates on me. "No, you can't be thinking that…" Carol just shakes her head at me.

HARV's holographic eyes pop open. "Zach, you do realize we are inside of SRIP right now," HARV lectures.

"I admit, it's a gamble," I think back.

"OK, why are you guys just staring at one another?" Maxx asks HARV, Carol, and me.

"They are communicating telepathically," Tezza remarks.

"What's so important you have to talk about it in secret?" Maxx asks.

"They are thinking which of us might be a killer," HAL50 says.

"True," I say holding up a finger. "But I'll bet credits to soy donuts I'm not thinking what you think."

"HARV, do you know where the control room is here?" I think.

"Of course."

A green glowing holographic arrow appears in front of my eyes. It points to a door toward the front of the ship. I start casually walking toward that door.

"Zach, where are you going?" Merinda asks.

"This ship is such a marvel. I really want to see the brains that hold everything together. It's not for me so much as it is for HARV."

HARV picks up on my lead and starts walking ahead of me. (There are advantages to being a hologram.) "Yes, this SRIP is *so* amazing!" HARV gushes. "I must see what makes it tick."

My hope now is that SRIP doesn't see where I'm going with this. But if my educated hunch is right and SRIP is the potential murderer here, then I have to make sure when I confront SRIP, I'm close enough to his brain to shut him down fast before he reacts.

"Passengers aboard, I am preparing to blast off. Please do *not* take your seats, as I wish to kill you all!" SRIP announces.

We feel and hear the ship's engines rumble and roar to life.

The good news is, my hunch about SRIP is right. The bad news is, SRIP is pretty sharp.

HARV, Carol, and I rush toward the control room. Merinda and her staff follow on our heels. Of course, SRIP continues to vibrate to life, which most likely means death to the rest of us.

"Zach, if this ship gets off the ground, you are doomed!" HARV says.

"Yeah, he'll probably fly us into the sun," HAL50 groans.

"No, the sun would take too long. I am going to crash you into the moon!" SRIP informs us.

Turning to Merinda's crew, I ask, "How long until SRIP can blast off?"

"The engines can go from cold to launch ready in four minutes and twenty-eight seconds," Tezza says proudly.

"Just lovely," I mumble.

"Hey, we can't help it if we're an efficient people," Tezza says.

We reach the door to the control room. Surprisingly, it opens right up for us. I hesitate.

"Oh, I thought this was going to be harder," I say.

"Yeah, this can't be a good sign," HARV says.

We enter the control room. It's a fairly unimpressive, seemingly empty room with glowing light-blue display panels lining the walls and the ceiling.

"Where are the main brains to this thing?" I ask.

Another glowing green arrow appears in front of my eyes. It points upward and then zooms up until it touches a spot on the ceiling.

"Shooting through this panel should totally disable SRIP," HARV tells me.

I pop my gun into my hand.

"Zach, are you sure of this?" Merinda asks.

"Unless SRIP powers down, I don't think there is another way," I tell her loudly.

The face of a young child with huge blue eyes and an angelic smile appears on the wall screens all around us.

"Greetings, Mr. Johnson, Merinda, Tezza, Maxxx, HAL50, Alicia, HARV, Carol, and, of course, Saturn!" the child says. "I have so enjoyed interacting with you all. I will take no pleasure in killing you."

Out of the corner of my eye, I notice a dozen little circular bots pop out of panels near the floor. The bots float into the air and start whizzing toward us.

"I've got the bots on the left," Carol tells me.

Carol glares at the charging bots and squeezes her fists. The bots crumble and crush like very weak soda cans in a vise. Carol opens her hands. The bots drop to the ground.

"Wow, what a woman!" Maxx says.

The bots on the right side continue buzzing toward me.

"Zach, there are six bots attacking you!" HARV tells me.

"Yeah, I see that," I say, spinning toward the bots. I fire six times. There are six explosions followed by six little bots shattering into many bot pieces.

"That's impressive!" Merinda says.

"The bullets are computer controlled," HARV informs her. "Zach basically just needed to count to six."

"Yeah, but I pulled the trigger with flare!" I say. Looking at SRIP's image, I say, "You tried taking us out with vacuum bots? That was your plan?"

SRIP's image shrugs. "You make do with what you are given."

I point my gun at the spot on the ceiling. "Stop stalling and power down, now!" I order.

"So, Mr. Johnson, it appears we are at an impasse!" the young child tells me.

"How much time do we have before SRIP is ready to launch?" I ask.

"One minute and seven seconds," HARV tells me.

I shake my head. "No impasse here, SRIP. You power down, or I shut you down for good!" There's a very slight pause to let what I said sink in. "HARV, let me know when SRIP is ten seconds from ignition."

"Check," HARV says.

"Yes, you could surely disable me, Mr. Johnson, but then you will never learn my motive or who programmed me to do this," SRIP says quickly.

OK, SRIP has a point here, but I don't have a lot of time to make a choice. I hold my gun steady, ready to take out SRIP in an instant. His offer, though, does intrigue me. After all, SRIP is just a tool here, a cog in the machine of death. He is not the one who started the process.

Then HARV tells me, "This is strange. You know how you wanted me to look for council member Sam Storm?"

"Yeah," I think back.

"I found him. He is in the rocket port actually looking at this rocket."

"So what will it be, Mr. Johnson?" SRIP prompts.

The image of Sam Storm appears in my head. He is smiling proudly and looking up at SRIP. I fire my gun.

SRIP goes blank and silent.

"Don't need you any longer!" I say to the dead screen.

"You don't care who's trying to kill us?" Tezza screams.

"I will contact Mars and have them send a new ship," Alicia says.

"Zach, are you sure about what you just did?" Merinda asks.

"Well he'd better be, 'cause there's no undoing it," HAL50 notes.

"Not unless Carol can rewind time," Maxxx says. He looks at her. "Can you?"

Carol shakes her head. "No, at least not yet."

I lower my gun and then state rather confidently with as much bravado as I can muster, "Yes, I've never been more sure." Pointing toward the outside of the now-terminated ship, I say, "The culprit behind all this is out there." I pause a moment for effect and then add, "It's Councilman Sam Storm."

I quickly head to the main section of the rocket. Everybody follows on my heels. Looking out one of the windows, Maxxx says, "Wait, if Councilman Storm is here, where's the security, the press, the aides?"

"He doesn't have any," I say, pressing toward the door.

"Then why isn't he being mobbed by people?" Merinda asks.

"Because he's traveling alone. Nobody recognizes him. After all, nobody here on Earth actually knows or cares what most of the Earth council members look like. To travel incognito, they merely need to travel alone. Sexy Sprockets once admitted to me that all she has to do to go old-fashioned store shopping in peace is take off her makeup and ditch the entourage. She hated the experience though."

"So you think Councilman Storm was the one who got SRIP to try to kill me?" Merinda asks me.

I nod. "You and all your people. To start an incident."

"Why? What motive does he have?" Tezza asks. "Mars has been nothing but helpful to Earth. Your people love our products." She smiles. "After all, they are of the highest quality! The best in all the worlds."

Continuing my way toward the door, I say, "Well, I am going to go ask him."

Carol leans forward and grabs me by the arm. "Zach, stop. You just can't go accuse a councilman of trying to kill a diplomat from Mars."

"Yes, what grounds do you have?" Merinda asks. "It would be your word against his."

"Yes, Zach, he would wriggle free for sure," HARV says.

"My gut tells me it's him," I growl.

HARV and Carol both shake their heads. "For the seventeenth time, your gut isn't admissible in court," HARV tells me.

I take a breath and then another. Deep down I know Sam Storm is the mastermind here. I can feel it in my bones. I remember his career as a pitcher. He didn't have great stuff, but he was tricky. Somehow, this all clicks with his Earth First Act. But contrary to popular belief, I'm not stupid. I know how the worlds work. If I go after Storm without any proof, he would skip away, free as a genetically enhanced free-range turchicken.

"HARV, find me something, anything to connect him to this," I say.

"On it," HARV says.

The question is, what am I going to do right now? Do I let Storm walk away without letting on that I am on to him? Or do I risk tipping my hand by confronting him?

need to go face-to-face with Sam Storm to catch him in the act. Well, not in the act, exactly, but watching the act he believes will lead to the death of one of the leaders of Mars. But first I need to get some sort of hint of evidence to confront him with.

"HARV, you gotta get me something to tie Sam Storm into SRIP's programming," I semiplead.

"I'm trying, Zach, but right now it might be easier to get me to talk Mars and the moon into becoming allies," HARV says.

"Hey, that's unfair!" Tezza protests. "We do some things with the moon. We can't help it if the mooners are arrogant snots."

"Wait, the moon did help with the SRIP interface. Right?" I say.

HARV nods. "Yes, that is one of the few times the moon and Mars have gotten along."

"They charged us a mint for that interface," Merinda says. "But it was worth it—kind of."

It hit me. SRIP had been planning to crash into the moon all along. The Earth First politician, Sam Storm, had wanted to start an incident between the moon and Mars all along. Of course, to do that he would have needed help—moon help.

"HARV, find me something—anything—to link Storm to somebody on the moon who helped program the SRIP interface. Storm was on the moon. Surely he had some contact with somebody from that team!"

HARV's eyes flash red. "Zach, I talked to Elena, and she gave me access to all the moon's security cameras. I got something! During his last trip there, Storm stayed in the same hotel as Sid Finch."

"So?"

"Finch is a low-level psi, but a high-level computer-interface engineer who was second-in-command in the SRIP project."

"That can't be a coincidence," Carol says.

"Well, it could be, but it most likely isn't," HARV notes. "Especially since he has reservations to come to Earth tomorrow."

"HARV, contact Elena. Have her find Sid and get a confession out of him. My guess is he's trying to move up his exit from the moon to today."

Yep, that's all I need. Not only was Finch on the moon when Storm was there, but he had also been planning to come to Earth just before SRIP had been originally planning to crash into the moon. I move to the door and say, "Time to go greet the good councilman."

"Do you want us to come with you?" Carol asks.

"I'd love to give that guy a piece of my mind!" Tezza says.

"I'll give him a piece of my fist," Maxxx says.

"I'll put him in a deep sleep!" Merinda says.

"Woof!" Saturn barks.

Heading out, I shake my head. "No, I don't want to spook him—at least not yet."

I walk up behind Storm, who is casually standing on a walkway, gazing up at SRIP.

"Fine ship, isn't it?" I say.

Storm nods. "It's an interesting ship. Of course, I prefer ones made on Earth."

"Yeah, but you can't get most Earth ships to fly into the moon, killing a member of the Mars Royal Council and starting an interplanetary incident," I say calmly.

Storm turns to me quickly. At first his eyes are wide open. He is surprised by what I said. His eyes narrow. He smiles. "Zachary Nixon Johnson," he says.

I nod. "In person. I'm surprised you recognize me."

"Actually," the council member says, "I'm surprised *you* recognized *me*."

"My computer pointed you out," I tell him.

"Ah, the legendary HARV," Storm says, catching me off guard. He knows more than I thought he would. "I assure you, Mr. Johnson, I have no idea what you are talking about."

"You know, normally when a politician says that, I believe it. But in this case, I think you know exactly what I meant. Maybe I should let the world know about your fondness for rockets and death?"

"Is that a threat, Mr. Johnson?" Storm asks.

"Yeah, pretty much." I shrug.

Storm casually grabs me by the shirt and easily lifts me off the ground with one hand. "I don't respond well to threats."

"Apparently, he is bionic," HARV says in my head.

"Yeah, I kind of figured that out," I respond to him mentally.

"So what's it like to be bionic?" I casually ask Storm while I weigh my options. "By the way, I hope you weren't bionic during your playing days, 'cause that would, one, be cheating, and two, it would be kind of sad, 'cause you weren't that good."

Storm laughs and shakes his head (and me a bit in the process). "To answer your questions in reverse order, the bionics are a result of my playing career, and I really do enjoy being bionic." He pauses for a moment to reflect. "At first I thought I'd miss my original arms, but I'll tell you something, Zach. Mind if I call you Zach?"

I shrug. "I'm cool with that."

"Well, Zach, I was special before the bionics, but the bionics made me more special. They took a near-perfect human specimen and made it better," the not-so-good councilman rambles.

"I'm happy for you," I tell him. "I truly am. But what is this all leading to?"

"Please, Mr. Johnson." He smiles. "I was building up to my point, but if you insist in rushing the process…"

Storm tosses me a good six meters through the air. I hit the ground with a hard thump.

"Well, you have confirmed he is bionic," HARV tells me.

I get up and spit some dirt out of my mouth.

"HARV, how's Elena coming along with tracking down that programmer?"

89

"Do you mean Sid Finch?"

"Yes, of course I do!"

"She says she found him at the moon port," HARV informs me, as Storm storms toward me.

"Good," I tell him. "Not sure how long I can keep this up without shooting him, and shooting a councilman without proof would not be a good career move."

"Zach, do you want my help?" Carol asks mentally.

"Not yet. This is between the councilman and me. I am going to try to get him to brag about his motive. I've got a better chance if he thinks he's about to kill me."

Storm punches a clenched fist into his palm. "This is going to feel so good, beating you!" He laughs.

Taking a fighting stance, I taunt, "Better politicians than you have tried."

Storm takes a big, lumbering swing at me. I see it coming from a kilometer away and duck under it. I pounce up and clock him with an uppercut to the jaw. He rocks back like one of those old Rock 'em Sock 'em Robots. I do so love when that happens. I could hit him with a combination to put him down, but I don't because I need him to talk. I want him angry but thinking he has the upper hand.

"Zach, I just learned something interesting about the not-so-good councilman," HARV tells me as I watch Storm stagger back.

"You gonna tell me, HARV?"

"He has been in top-secret talks with *Worlds News Right Now*. It looks like he's planning on becoming a news reporter."

Storm recovers his balance and then staggers forward, throwing a bionic right cross at me, which I easily block. That's one of the advantages of having underarmor and a computer wired to my brain. I can take more damage than the average Joe. From the look on Storm's face, I can tell he's surprised I stopped his blow so easily. As Storm's punch fails, something clicks in my brain. I know what Storm is up to. He doesn't just want to start a war between the moon and Mars. He wants to start a war and then cover it for the news. So this would be a win-win for him. Of course, there is no way I am going to let him get away with this. I wasn't about to let the fact that I still only had very circumstantial evidence on Storm slow me down.

Storm lunges at me, putting me in a bear hug. "I'll crush the air out of your lungs!" he tells me. "I will tell the world you threatened me with blackmail!"

Now that Storm thought he had the upper hand on me, in his arrogance I could probably get him to admit his wrongdoing. After all, politicians and criminals both love to brag, and Storm is both.

"Zach, Elena has Finch under control. She will be teleporting down any minute!" HARV informs me.

"Zach, I can't stand by any longer. I'm going to come out there now and put a mental beating on that arrogant Storm!" Merinda thinks at me.

OK, now this could complicate matters. While having either Elena or Merinda on my side could be quite the asset, I was afraid if they both tried to help, they might end up at each other's throats.

Storm tightens his bear hug on me, making it harder to breathe. "I'll crush the air out of your lungs!" he repeats. "You will die a criminal for attacking a councilman! You are a mere ant for thinking you could get in my way!"

"That doesn't make a lot of sense," I tell him. "But I guess asking for sense from a politician is just asking for too much."

"Zach, Merinda and Elena really want to help!" HARV tells me in my brain.

"Let me get a bit more of a confession out of Storm. Now that he thinks he has the upper hand, I am sure he'll brag some—"

Looking Storm in the eyes, I say, "So you got those cleaning bots and those security drones to attack me."

Storm glares at me as he tightens his grip. "Of course it was me, you fool! My old company made those bots. It was easy to reprogram them. I couldn't take the chance of you interfering with my plans!"

OK, now that I had gotten him to talk, it was time to let my psi friends go at him. I had drawn him out, and now I should let them have the pleasure of finishing him off. After all, with Merinda being from Mars and Elena being from the moon, they had the most at stake here.

"Bring 'em in, HARV!" I say out loud.

I accent my words by clamping my fists hard into Storm's ears. The intensity of my blow forces Storm to release his bear hug on me. Stumbling to the ground but remaining on my feet, I make a fist and show it to Storm.

Out of the corner of my eye, I see Merinda storming at us from one side. She has Carol and the rest of her posse close behind. I also see Elena teleporting in behind us. She has a skinny man with a beard following her. He is on all fours and panting like a dog. Yeah, you don't want to make Elena mad.

"How dare you hurt a councilman!" Storm roars at me. "You'll spend the rest of your little life in prison for that."

I point to Elena and Merinda closing in on us. "Ah, don't think so. Not when my psi friends are here to make you sing the truth."

Storm laughs. "I'll just tell people they mind-washed me into talking! I'm loved. My popularity rating in nearly 13%! People will never believe I started a war between Mars and the moon!"

"Dude, one, the evidence will prove you did start the war. And two, I've just recorded you saying that, including you admitting to wanting to kill me. And that was before Elena and Merinda were here."

"And I feel obligated to point out that 13% is not very high," HARV adds.

Storm stood there taking in our words. Acting like the politician he was, he decides to make a run for it. I wasn't going to let that happen, though, especially since he's dense enough to try to run past me. I simply stick out my leg and let him trip over it. He makes a very clumsy headfirst dive in the mud.

"You ass!" he mumbles, his face still in the dirt. He starts pushing himself up from the ground.

Elena ports herself (and what appears to be her pet man) right next to the fallen councilman. She puts a purple boot on his back. "Stay down!" she orders. "I am taking you to the moon for prosecution!"

The councilman stops pushing upward and drops to the ground. "You have no proof!" he groans.

Elena turns to the man she has on a leash. "Speak!" she orders.

"Woof!" he barks obediently.

"Speak words!" Elena orders the man.

"Storm paid me to reprogram the SRIP computer system to crash into the moon," the man says.

"Very good," Elena tells him with a pat on the head. "Now, go back to being a dog!"

The man obediently rolls over.

Elena points dramatically at Storm. "Like I said, I'm taking you to the moon!"

By this time, Merinda and the others have reached us. At first I'm surprised nobody else seems to be paying attention to the commotion. Then I realize everybody around us who's not us is sleeping.

"No, Elena. I insist we take him to Mars for punishment!" Merinda says, walking up next to Elena.

"So why'd you do it, Storm?" I ask; I am quite sure I know the answer, but I want him to say it.

"I'll never tell you!" Storm growls.

"Tell him!" Elena, Merinda, and Carol order.

"Well, as you know, I've been a fan of Earth First. I thought putting Mars and the moon at each other's throats by either having the moon kill one of the Mars leaders or by crashing the ship into the moon, which would have been great for Earth! Not only that, but since I am retiring from politics and going into new media, this would be an amazing story to cover!"

So there we have it. The typical greedy politician wants everything his way.

Elena and Merinda lock eyes with each other. "He's mine!" they both say.

"Ladies, I think I might have a solution. Since Storm is guilty but nobody innocent got hurt—"

"Well, our SRIP got reprogrammed!" Tezza points out.

"Well, yeah, but it can be un-reprogrammed," I say.

They all nod. "Which brings me back to the not-so-good councilman. I agree if you leave him on Earth, he may not get the punishment he deserves. But if either of you takes him, it could start an incident."

They all look at me with tilted heads and open eyes, so I go on. "I think you should let him retire, but reprogram *him* to do something useful with his life, like help feed the poor or walk nonrobotic dogs."

They all smile.

"That's an outrage!" Storm barks. He stops barking. He smiles from the ground.

EPILOGUE

After saying our good-byes, Elena actually gave Merinda and her crew a teleport back to the moon. (Elena and Saturn hit it off right away. Elena always did have a soft spot for dogs and turnips.) From there they would discuss a new moon-Mars treaty and then catch a shuttle back to Mars. The now-good councilman announced his immediate retirement from politics to go live in the South Pole and begin work to save sick penguins. As for Sid Finch, I understand his new position would be Elena's permanent foot massager.

Driving home, Carol leans over toward me from the passenger seat. "So you're cool letting the councilman go?" she asks.

I nod. "Yeah, he could have done grave damage, but we stopped him, thanks to a mind-reading dog. Now, he's a changed person—a better person. The world may not be better for it but it's no worse. Sometimes you break even and call it a win. And well, justice was served."

HARV appears in my dash. "Actually, Zach, for you, this case was fairly low stakes. You just saved the moon and Mars from a messy possible war. Normally you save the Earth from being destroyed!"

"No reason why I can't have an easy case once in a while," I tell him. I smile, knowing that my next case probably will be direr. But for now I'm just going to enjoy the ride home.

www.ingramcontent.com/pod-product-compliance
Lightning Source LLC
Chambersburg PA
CBHW071335130626
46556CB00004B/1907